MANDIE
AND THE
ANGEL'S
SECRET

Mandie Mysteries

Mandie's Cookbook

MANDIE
AND THE
ANGEL'S
SECRET

Lois Gladys Leppard

BETHANY HOUSE PUBLISHERS
MINNEAPOLIS, MINNESOTA 55438

Mandie and the Angel's Secret
Lois Gladys Leppard

All scripture quotations are taken from the
King James Version of the Bible.

Library of Congress Catalog Card Number 93–72044

ISBN 1–55661–370–9

Published by Bethany House Publishers
A Ministry of Bethany Fellowship, Inc.
11300 Hampshire Avenue South
Minneapolis, Minnesota 55438

Printed in the United States of America

In remembrance of my fourth grade teacher, Miss Laura Butler, who required her students to memorize this wonderful poem, which has stayed with me all these years.

Abou Ben Adhem

Abou Ben Adhem, may his tribe increase!
Awoke one night from a deep dream of peace,
And saw, within the moonlight in his room,
Making it rich, and like a lily in bloom,
An Angel writing in a book of gold;
Exceeding peace had made Ben Adhem bold,
And to the Presence in the room he said,
"What writest thou?" The Vision raised its head,
And with a look made of all sweet accord
Answered, "The names of those who love the Lord."
"And is mine one?" said Abou. "Nay, not so,"
Replied the Angel. Abou spoke more low,
But cheerily still; and said, "I pray thee, then,
Write me as one that loves his fellowmen."
The Angel wrote, and vanished. The next night
It came again with a great wakening light,
And showed the names whom the love of God had
    blessed,
And, lo! Ben Adhem's name led all the rest!

James Henry Leigh Hunt
(1784–1859)

About the Author

LOIS GLADYS LEPPARD has been a Federal Civil Service employee in various countries around the world. She makes her home in South Carolina.

The stories of her own mother's childhood are the basis for many of the incidents incorporated in this series.

Contents

"And there appeared an angel unto him from heaven, strengthening him."

Luke 22:43

Chapter 1 / Goodbye, Jonathan!

Mandie and Celia overslept their last morning in London. If Molly had not climbed into bed with them, they wouldn't have been dressed by the time Mrs. Taft was ready for breakfast. Even at that, they only had a few minutes to quickly slip into their traveling clothes in preparation for their long journey back to the United States.

"Molly, I'm so glad you woke us up," Mandie said, handing the Irish orphan a dress. "And I'm so glad that Grandmother agreed to take you home with us until we can locate your aunt in the United States." She tied the girl's sash.

"That I be, too," Molly replied with a big grin. Mandie quickly brushed Molly's carrot-colored hair. "And I've changed me mind, I have. And glad I'll be if ye niver find that aunt of mine in United States so's I kin live with ye."

Mandie hurriedly tied a ribbon in Molly's long hair, and stepped back to shake out her own long skirts. She looked at Molly and silently worried about what would happen to the girl if they didn't locate her aunt. She knew Molly's parents were both dead and that she had been living with Mrs. Riley, her mother's friend, but because of a terrible accident the woman could no longer give the girl a home.

Celia, buttoning her shoes, looked across the room at Mandie and then at Molly. "Oh, but, Molly, your aunt is real blood kin to you. She's your mother's sister; remember, we explained all that," she told the girl.

"Kin or no, I've niver seen her in all me born days," Molly said with a shrug as she pranced around the room.

Mandie laughed and said, "That's not very long. You won't be ten till September the first."

Mrs. Taft opened the door across the sitting room and came out of her bedroom in a hurry.

"Amanda! Celia! Get Molly and let's hurry down to breakfast," she told them as she kept going out into the corridor.

"Coming, Grandmother," Mandie called after her. She scooped up her white kitten, Snowball, and fastened on his red leash.

Celia took Molly's hand and they rushed after Mrs. Taft, who was almost out of sight down the hallway.

When they arrived at the hotel dining room, Jonathan and his father, Lindall Guyer, and Senator Morton were already seated at a table near the front window. Mrs. Taft led the way across the room and the men rose to greet them.

Mandie quickly tied Snowball's leash to the table leg and sat down between Celia and Jonathan. Senator Morton pulled out a chair for Molly and waited for her to sit down.

"Where is Uncle Ned?" Mandie asked as she glanced around the table. Her father's old Cherokee friend was absent. Before Jim Shaw died the year before, Uncle Ned had promised her father he'd watch over Mandie. So he had been traveling with them throughout Europe.

"He had a last-minute errand, Amanda," Senator Morton told her with a smile. "He'll join us shortly."

"Have y'all ordered your breakfast yet?" Mrs. Taft asked.

Senator Morton's blue eyes twinkled as he replied with a smile, "Oh, yes. We told them to bring some of everything since we didn't know what everyone wanted and we are pushed for time."

At that moment the waiter rolled a loaded tea cart to their table and began placing dishes of hot food before them. The three young people deeply inhaled the aroma and Molly rolled her eyes in eager anticipation.

Uncle Ned came hurrying up to the table and sat down across from Mandie.

"You're right on time," Mandie said with a laugh. "Good morning, Uncle Ned. Did you get your errand done?"

Uncle Ned glanced across the table at her and then turned to the dishes being passed around. "Yes, Papoose, all done," he said.

"Amanda, Celia, eat your food now. We've got to get going to the ship in just a little while," Mrs. Taft told the girls as she looked at Uncle Ned.

Mandie quickly began to butter a hot roll, but she happened to look up in time to see some kind of silent communication going on between her grandmother and Uncle Ned. Mrs. Taft raised her eyebrows and pursed her lips as she looked at the old Indian. Uncle Ned slowly nodded his head in the affirmative. Mandie glanced at Mr. Guyer and Senator Morton. They were both beginning to eat and didn't seem aware of the exchange between her grandmother and Uncle Ned.

Mandie wondered to herself what was going on. Why was everyone acting so secretive? And what was Uncle Ned's errand? He hadn't volunteered any information. She didn't like being left out of a secret, and evidently some kind of secret was being kept from her.

"Jonathan, we're going to miss you on our trip home," Celia said, looking around Mandie to the boy.

"Yeah, me too. I wish I could sail with all of you, but you know I'd much rather go with my father to Paris," Jonathan replied with his mischievous grin.

Mandie looked at him. They had met up with Jonathan Guyer on their way to Europe. Her grandmother, Mrs. Taft, and their family friend, Senator Morton, had taken her and Celia Hamilton on the journey while school back in North Carolina was out during the summer of 1901. Her grandmother had suddenly decided to cut the trip short while they were in Ireland, and now they were going home.

"We *are* going to miss you, Jonathan, but I'm so glad you finally caught up with your father," Mandie told him. "And I've enjoyed every minute of our various adventures." She leaned over to place a saucer of food under the table for Snowball.

"So have I," Jonathan said as he continued eating from his heaped plate of food. "We just have to get together sometime soon when we all get home."

"New York is a long way from where we live; with Mandie in North Carolina and me in Virginia," Celia said with a sigh.

"Oh, but there is a train that goes all the way to New York," Jonathan said, again grinning at the two girls.

"And there's a train that comes all the way from New York to Virginia and North Carolina," Mandie said with a laugh. She glanced at her grandmother and Uncle Ned.

They were not even looking at each other now.

"Well, I'll come down to visit you girls if you will come to New York to my house," Jonathan said, hastily drinking his coffee.

Mrs. Taft spoke up, "We'll see, Jonathan. Now please eat your breakfast, girls. Even Molly is finishing off her food."

Mandie hadn't realized that her grandmother had been listening to their conversation. She looked at Molly and saw that she was almost finished. The girl was not used to such good, plentiful food, and Mandie was thankful they had been given the opportunity to help her.

"I suppose I forgot to mention it, Amanda, but after we arrived yesterday I sent out for some more clothes for Molly and a trunk to put them in. She could hardly spend all this time on the ship home with the two dresses I bought her in Ireland," Mrs. Taft told Mandie. "Her trunk will be put in the rooms on the ship with yours and Celia's."

Mandie smiled at her grandmother and said, "Thank you, Grandmother. I didn't even think about clothes for her." She turned to Molly, who had heard the conversation and who was now looking sternly at Mrs. Taft. "More new clothes, Molly," Mandie said. "Aren't you glad?"

"Aye, but how will I ever get such finery paid for?" Molly said with a worried frown.

Everyone at the table laughed at her innocent remark.

"Oh, but, Molly, I am giving these clothes to you. You don't owe me anything for them," Mrs. Taft tried to explain.

Molly didn't reply and Mandie said, "You are getting all these new clothes because we love you and want you to be happy."

"If bein' happy is all I owed yawl, then ye kin consider

me bill paid," Molly said, finally grinning as she clasped her hands together beneath her chin.

Mr. Guyer looked at Molly from down the table and said, "Molly, after you go to live with your aunt in the United States, I want you to bring her to see Jonathan and me. Will you promise me that?" He smiled.

"I don't be knowin' the direction to take. Could I bring Mandie with me to show me the way?" Molly asked, anxiously looking at Mandie.

"Of course, Molly, bring Mandie and everyone—her grandmother, Celia, Uncle Ned, Senator Morton, and anyone else who wants to come," Mr. Guyer replied.

Mandie saw her grandmother frown. "We'll have to decide about such a trip later," Mrs. Taft told Mr. Guyer.

Mr. Guyer quickly caught his breath and said, "I understand. When all your troubles have subsided we'd love to have you, every one of you."

Mrs. Taft hurriedly looked around the table and said, "I believe we're all finished now. Let's freshen up in our rooms. Senator Morton has a carriage waiting to take us to the ship, so we must hurry." She stood up and everyone else did likewise. "Amanda, Celia, please be sure you don't leave anything in your rooms."

"Yes, ma'am," the girls chorused.

Mandie untied Snowball's leash and picked him up. He had licked his saucer clean.

There was no time for conversation in the hallway on the way to their rooms, but once Mandie and Celia and Molly entered their bedroom and closed the door to keep Snowball from going out, Mandie turned quickly to her friend and asked, "Did you hear that remark Mr. Guyer made about going to visit after all our troubles have subsided? Celia, I'm worried about my grandmother. Do you think she might be sick?"

Celia reached for Mandie's hand and said, "No, I don't think she's sick, Mandie. I think she's just tired and in a hurry to get home and all."

Mandie looked at her friend again and said, "But she's kinda old, you know, Celia, and this trip might have been too much for her."

"Mandie, if you stop to think, you'll remember that your grandmother has taken time to rest whenever she wanted to, and other than that she has kept right up with everyone else. She may be getting old but she's not *that* old," Celia replied.

Molly was standing nearby trying to understand what the girls were talking about. Now she said, "Mandie, Grandmother said for us to freshen up. How do we be doin' that?"

Mandie and Celia laughed and took Molly into the bathroom.

"You just take a clean washcloth, wet it like this, and wash your face and hands; but be careful not to get your dress wet," Mandie explained. She handed Molly the wet cloth and watched as the girl hurriedly did as she was told.

Celia reached for a clean towel and handed it to Molly. "Then you dry off with this," Celia explained.

Molly dried off and watched as the two girls freshened up.

There was a tap on their bedroom door and Mrs. Taft called to them, "Ready, girls?"

"Yes, Grandmother," Mandie said as she rushed to open the door, then picked up her purse and Snowball. Celia grabbed her things and took Molly's hand.

Mrs. Taft stuck her head inside to look around the room.

"The men took our luggage while we were eating

breakfast. I hope you girls got everything else," she said as she turned to go to the hallway door.

"We did, Grandmother," Mandie assured her.

As they stepped into the corridor they were joined by Jonathan and his father.

"We're going to the ship with you and then we'll be leaving in about two hours to go to Paris," Jonathan told the girls as he fell in beside them.

"You're going to get on the ship with us?" Mandie questioned.

"That's right. That is if you girls don't mind," Jonathan said with his mischievous grin.

"We might stow you away," Mandie teased. "Remember, we did that before."

"I remember very well," Jonathan replied. "At least this time you won't have that strange woman on the ship with you."

"She caused us a lot of trouble on the ship coming over, didn't she?" Celia said.

"She sure did," Mandie agreed. She glanced at Molly by her side. "I suppose Molly will be replacing you this time, Jonathan."

"Maybe there'll be another time. I hope so, anyway," Jonathan told the girls with an unusually solemn look on his face.

When they stepped outside the hotel, Mandie saw Uncle Ned and Senator Morton standing by the waiting carriage. Another vehicle stood behind theirs and Mr. Guyer went directly to it.

"Come along, Jonathan. This one is ours until we are ready to leave on our journey," Mr. Guyer told the boy.

The two quickly boarded their carriage as the others piled into the one Senator Morton had secured.

"I suppose it would have been a close fit if we had all

tried to ride in this one, wouldn't it," Mandie said to Celia as they helped Molly up onto the seat by the window. She had noticed their hatboxes and small bags on the floor.

Mrs. Taft heard the remark and explained, "We didn't want our bags put outside on the rack, dear. It looks as though it might rain and it's quicker and safer to have them inside with us."

"Besides, Lindall Guyer had already rented his carriage for their stay here," Senator Morton added.

Mandie silently thought about this. Her grandmother seemed to avoid Mr. Guyer if at all possible. She wondered why.

When they arrived at the wharf, Mandie and Celia noted with surprise that their ship was the *Queen Victoria*, which they had sailed on from the United States.

Upon seeing the name, Mandie paused to say, "Look, we're going back on the same ship. Do you suppose there aren't any other ships sailing to the United States?" Mandie turned to look at Celia as they followed Mrs. Taft and Senator Morton up the gangplank. Mandie held tightly to Snowball, and Celia squeezed Molly's hand in hers.

Before Celia could answer, Molly had pulled backward and halted. She asked, "Do we be havin' to ride on this big ship?"

Mandie stopped and looked at her. "Come on, Molly. This ship is like a house inside. We came to Europe on it," she told the girl.

Molly stood still on the gangplank as passengers rushed around her. She looked up at Mandie and then at Celia. "With a bed and everything?" Molly asked.

"Of course. We will be living on this ship for days and days. It takes a long time to get to the United States. It's all the way across the ocean," Mandie explained. "Now come on, Molly. We're going to lose Grandmother, she's so far ahead of us."

Molly still wouldn't budge. "No, me thinks me would like to go back to Belfast," she said.

"And give up all those pretty clothes Mrs. Taft bought you?" Celia asked.

"Yes, and I heard you call her 'Grandmother,' " Mandie told her. "Well, if you are going to be her granddaughter you have to go where she goes."

"I do?" Molly asked, looking up the gangplank.

"Of course. She's going back to the United States whether you go or not. Now, are you coming with us?" Mandie asked.

Molly sighed deeply and shrugged her thin shoulders. Without a word she continued on her way up the gangplank with Celia holding tightly to her hand. Mandie looked at Celia over Molly's head and smiled.

They caught up with Mrs. Taft, Senator Morton, and Uncle Ned as they stepped on deck. Mandie wondered where Jonathan and his father were. When they finally got to their rooms, the girls found Jonathan and his father waiting for them along with quite a few other people who were evidently friends of Mrs. Taft and Senator Morton. They had a suite of four rooms this time, with a small sitting room between the girls' and Mrs. Taft's rooms. A single room for Molly adjoined Mandie and Celia's.

"Took you long enough to get here," Jonathan teased as the girls entered the sitting room.

Mandie tied Snowball's leash to a door handle and looked around to find Molly exploring the suite of rooms. "Molly decided she didn't want to get on this ship and we had to coax her," Mandie explained.

"Look at all the food!" Celia remarked as she saw a laden table through the crowd of adults.

"Food?" Jonathan quickly asked as he moved toward the table. "Come on. There's candy, cookies, coffee, milk—everything. Let's sample all of it." He continued to work his way through the crowd until he reached the food.

Mandie and Celia followed him. "But we just got through eating breakfast, Jonathan. How can you eat more now?" Mandie asked as she watched him piling cookies onto a napkin.

Jonathan looked at her with his mischievous grin and said, "I can always eat. If I don't eat all this now, I'll save it for my journey to Paris with my father. We may not be so lucky on that trip."

Mandie laughed and picked up one cookie to nibble at. Celia took a small glass of milk. But when Molly spotted the food, she began hastily cramming cookies into her pockets.

"Molly, you don't have to do that. These are our rooms and they'll leave all this here for us. If you put cookies in your pockets they'll get all crumbled and soil your pretty dress," Mandie explained as she stooped to reach for the crushed cookies.

"Then they be havin' food to eat on this big ship?" Molly asked in surprise as she allowed Mandie to clean out her pockets.

"Oh, lots of it, more than we can ever eat," Mandie assured her as she put the crumbs in a napkin and laid it on the table. "They'll have breakfast every morning and a meal at noontime and a big, big meal at night." She stepped back and straightened her long skirts. "Now, just take one cookie at a time. You can eat all you want, but only one at a time. You understand?"

Molly shrugged, snatched a crumbled cookie from the napkin, and crammed it into her mouth as she glanced toward Mandie. "Kin I be havin' a wee bit of that milk?" she asked as she looked at the filled glasses on the table.

"Of course, but please be careful, Molly, and don't spill it on your new dress," Mandie said, reaching to hand her a glass that was very full.

At that moment the ship's horn sounded. The young people jumped in surprise and then they all laughed.

"That's the warning for all of us visitors to go ashore," Jonathan told the girls. "Are you coming out to the deck so I can wave goodbye to you from the wharf?"

"Of course, Jonathan," Mandie said. "Come on, Molly, I can't leave you here alone. Everyone is going outside to see the ship start sailing." Molly finished her milk and set the glass back on the table.

The deck was crowded, and Mandie and Celia stopped to tell Jonathan goodbye before finding a place at the rail to wave to him. Celia held tightly to Molly's hand.

Mandie suddenly felt a lump in her throat and her eyes threatened to fill with tears as she realized her friendship with Jonathan was over, for the time being at least. They were all going to destinations hundreds and hundreds of miles apart.

"Jonathan, I hope—I wish—oh, you know what I mean. Write to us," Mandie said quickly, dropping her eyes.

Jonathan surprised her by suddenly reaching for her hand and saying, "Mandie, look at me. I will. I promise I will," he said, solemnly looking into her blue eyes. "And I promise we'll see each other again—sometime, some-where." He turned to Celia and added, "I'll see you, too, Celia. Be good." And he quickly disappeared in the direction his father had gone.

Mandie pulled her handkerchief from her purse and quickly dabbed at her eyes while Celia led Molly toward the rail.

"Over here, Mandie. I see your grandmother and Senator Morton, but I don't see Uncle Ned," Celia said as she pushed her way through the crowd.

Mandie followed as she sniffed, and straightened her shoulders. She asked herself why she had to make such a scene in front of Jonathan. He was just another friend. And she had lots of friends. She imagined Jonathan thought she was silly acting that way.

Celia and Molly had gotten ahead of Mandie, when she suddenly bumped into someone. She looked up to see Uncle Ned smiling down at her. She blinked her eyes. She certainly didn't want Uncle Ned to see her crying.

"Oh, Uncle Ned," she said softly as he put his arm around her and led her to the rail.

The two stood there, silently watching the people below. Finally Mandie sighted Jonathan and his father. Jonathan's eyes had found her, and he was waving and yelling something Mandie couldn't understand from the distance, and then suddenly he threw her a kiss with his hand.

Mandie began waving vigorously with her lace handkerchief, and somehow it slipped from her fingers and went sailing through the air toward the crowd below. She held her breath and watched as Jonathan pushed people aside and jumped into the air to catch it. She saw him hold it to his face to smell it and then wave to her with the lacy piece of cloth.

Mandie looked up at Uncle Ned with a smile and said, "Oh, well, I have another one in my trunk."

"Yes, but that one special, Papoose," Uncle Ned said, smiling and holding her hand. "Jonathan boy keep that one close to heart."

Trying to cover her emotion, Mandie said with a little laugh, "Jonathan probably keeps all girls' handkerchiefs close to his heart."

The ship sounded its last call and Mandie could feel the huge vessel tremble as it began to move. Another rush of emotion passed over her as she realized she was finally on the way home—to her mother, Uncle John, who had married her mother when her father died, and her little baby brother, Samuel.

She looked up at her tall friend and said happily, "We're going home, Uncle Ned. I can't wait to see my mother, Uncle John, and my baby brother. I imagine he has grown a lot since we've been gone."

Uncle Ned did not reply but put his arm around her and held her tight.

Chapter 2 / Sailing Home

"Senator Morton and I are going inside for a cup of tea," Mrs. Taft told Mandie and Celia. "Do you all want to come with us? Uncle Ned?" She looked up at the old Indian as the crowds of passengers hurried toward the doorways.

"Grandmother, could we please stay out here a little while?" Mandie asked as she looked at Celia, who nodded in agreement.

"I watch over Papoose," Uncle Ned said.

"Well, it's getting awfully windy out here and I'm sure it's going to rain, so don't stay outside too long," Mrs. Taft said. "We'll be in the first tearoom on the left if you look for us." She and Senator Morton walked on toward the line of people going inside.

"Yes, ma'am," Mandie said. She leaned over to speak to Molly, who was clinging to Celia, and asked, "Do you want to walk around the deck with us?"

Molly asked as she stared about, "Where be this 'deck'?"

"That's what we're standing on right now. You see, it goes 'way down yonder, clear out of sight around the bend," Mandie explained as she pointed ahead.

"No, that be too far on this wobbly ship. Right here I stay. You do the walkin'," Molly said, vigorously shaking her carrot-topped head.

Uncle Ned smiled at Molly and stooped to take her hand from Celia's. "I sit with Papoose Molly and wait," he said, leading the girl toward a row of deck chairs nearby.

"Thank you, Uncle Ned," Mandie said as she and Celia turned to walk down the deck. "We won't be gone long," Mandie called back to him.

"Do you think Jonathan will write to us?" Celia asked.

Mandie quickly looked at her friend. Was Celia personally interested in Jonathan? Instances of Jonathan comforting Celia during some of their scary adventures flipped through Mandie's mind. Was Jonathan personally interested in Celia?

"Well?" Celia asked as she looked at Mandie.

"Oh," Mandie said, quickly coming back to Celia's question. "I suppose he will. He said he would."

"He's different from other boys we've known, don't you think?" Celia asked. They moved on through the thinning crowd on deck.

"I suppose so," Mandie said, making a nervous gesture with her hands.

"I hope he writes. I'd like to go to New York to see him, too," Celia told her.

"I would, too," Mandie quickly asserted. "But then I'll have to wait until my grandmother agrees to take me." She glanced at Celia again.

"Whenever you do go, Mandie, could I go with y'all?" Celia asked, smiling as she paused to put her hand on Mandie's arm.

Mandie walked a step or two and then turned to say,

"Of course, Celia. But I think we'd better go back now. I'd like to have a cup of tea with my grandmother. How about you?"

"That sounds good," Celia agreed.

The girls rejoined Uncle Ned and Molly and they all went inside in search of the tearoom. Mandie immediately spotted her grandmother with her head bent toward Senator Morton in what seemed like a serious conversation. Mandie hurried to their table. Uncle Ned and Celia followed, with Molly clinging to Ned.

"Grandmother, we decided we did want some tea after all," Mandie said, causing her grandmother to look up, suddenly aware of their presence.

"Then sit down, dear," Mrs. Taft told her, motioning for the others to join her and the senator.

After they had all been seated and had been served tea and biscuits, Mandie tried to start a conversation but everyone seemed disinclined to talk.

"It was windy outside," Mandie remarked as she looked at her grandmother.

Mrs. Taft slowly sipped her tea and replied, "Yes, and it's going to rain. And I'm afraid I'm not very seaworthy in a storm." She smiled at Mandie.

"Do you think we'll be going into a storm?" Mandie asked anxiously as she thought about storms at sea. They had run into a storm in the middle of the night on their way to Europe in the same ship. Mandie had been frightened. After all, she didn't even know how to swim.

"We might, but don't worry about that, dear. This ship is safe," Mrs. Taft told her. "It's just the violent motions of the ship in a storm that upset me."

At that moment a short, plump, elderly man stopped by their table. "Well, this is a nice surprise, Senator Morton, to see you on this ship. I was worried about talking to myself all the way home and now here you are," he said, jovially extending his hand to the senator.

Senator Morton stood, shook hands, and said, "Mrs. Taft, may I present my friend here, Mr. Rodney Gifford. He's in the fruit-growing business in Florida." As Mrs. Taft rose, Senator Morton added, "And Rodney, this is Mrs. Taft, Senator Norman Taft's widow."

"Oh, indeed," Mr. Gifford said, quickly nodding his head. "I knew your husband, Mrs. Taft. It's a pleasure to meet you."

"The pleasure is mine, Mr. Gifford, and with no reflection on you, if you gentlemen will excuse me, I think I'll retire to my cabin. I need a little rest before the noon meal is served," Mrs. Taft replied.

Mandie looked anxiously at her grandmother. "Grandmother, are you sick? Is there anything I can do for you?" she asked as she, too, rose from the table.

"No, no, dear. I'm not sick, just tired. You just stay here with your friends and I'll see you all in the dining room later," Mrs. Taft insisted as she prepared to leave the room. "It was nice meeting you, Mr. Gifford."

"I hope our paths cross again, Mrs. Taft, and that you are fully rested by mealtime," Mr. Gifford told her, with a slight bow and a big smile.

At the doorway, Mrs. Taft called back to Mandie, "Amanda, you should check on that cat. You've left him tied to your door all this time."

"Oh, yes, ma'am, how could I have forgotten," Mandie said with a sigh as she followed her grandmother. "I'll be right back, Celia. I'll bring Snowball and we can walk around a while."

"All right, I'll wait here," Celia agreed.

Senator Morton and Mr. Gifford left to discuss politics in the smoking lounge, and Uncle Ned stayed with Molly, who had been silently listening.

Mrs. Taft told Mandie she would see her at mealtime

and went into her room. Mandie rushed into her own room to rescue Snowball from where he had been tied to the doorknob.

"Oh, Snowball, I'm sorry," Mandie told him as she untied his leash. "Come on. We'll go for some exercise." Snowball meowed loudly and rubbed against her long skirts.

Mandie glanced at her grandmother's closed door as she took Snowball and left the room. She didn't care what excuses Mrs. Taft made, she believed her grandmother was ill. Mandie could see she was not her usual energetic self. She sighed as she led Snowball down the corridor. She'd be so glad when they were finally home again!

Molly refused to walk around with Mandie and Celia on the "big wobbly ship," and Uncle Ned again volunteered to keep her with him, and they decided to go to the game room.

The two girls pushed their bonnets back and let them hang from the strings. Then they wandered about the corridors and discussed their journey to Europe on the same ship.

"I wish Violet and Lily were with us on this trip home," Mandie remarked as they walked down a long corridor. They had met the girls on their way to Europe. "It's going to be pretty lonely without them, and without Jonathan, too, isn't it?"

"Definitely," Celia agreed. "And just think, we won't have that strange woman following us around this time."

"Maybe we'll meet someone new," Mandie said, pulling on Snowball's leash as he tried to run ahead.

"I suppose we should catch up on our journals while we're on this ship. We haven't been writing everything down and we may forget half of it if we don't record it pretty soon," Celia reminded Mandie.

"Oh, I couldn't forget all the adventures we've had

since we left home. Never," Mandie said with a laugh. "But it will take a lot of paper to write it all down."

At that moment, Snowball tugged hard and managed to escape from Mandie's hold on his leash. He scampered down the corridor and the girls hurried after him.

"Snowball, come back here!" Mandie called as he rounded a corner.

Mandie caught up to him and leaned down to grab the wayward kitten, when she suddenly collided with a pair of legs. Celia almost bumped into Mandie when she stopped. They straightened up to look into the face of Charles, the British steward who had served their rooms on the way to Europe. Mandie and Celia both thought he was handsome.

"Well, cheerio there!" Charles said. "And how are you?" He smiled, showing his perfect set of glistening white teeth. "Does this cat belong to you?"

Mandie finally noticed that he was holding on to the end of Snowball's leash. She quickly took it from him as Snowball tried to pull free.

"Thank you," Mandie said. "Please forgive me for bumping into you, but Snowball here has a habit of running away and disappearing, and my grandmother would be awfully upset if we didn't find him right away. She's in her cabin resting right now, and Uncle Ned is looking after Molly, and Celia and I thought we would just go for a walk through the ship." She stopped, out of breath and definitely discombobulated at the sudden appearance of Charles.

Charles was still smiling as he replied, "I understand, Miss. If you need anything, please call. I am your steward on your journey back to the United States." He nodded and continued on his way down the corridor.

"Well, what do you know?" Mandie said, watching Charles disappear around the next corner. "We do know somebody on the ship this time."

"Right, and I imagine there are a lot of other employees who sailed with us last time," Celia told her.

"I suppose so," Mandie agreed as she tugged at Snowball's leash. "Come on, Snowball, this way." Turning back to Celia, she said, "Let's walk outside on the deck."

"We'd better put on our bonnets first," Celia said, pulling hers up off her shoulders and tying it securely under her chin.

Mandie laid Snowball's leash on the floor and put her foot firmly on it while she tied her bonnet. "Ready," she said, picking up the cat's leash.

The girls went out the doorway near their cabin. Mandie looked around the deck. Very few people were outside, probably because it was cloudy and the wind was blowing. One man sat in a deck chair against the wall as he read a book. Farther on, Mandie noticed a young woman in another chair trying to knit as the wind tangled her yarn. Suddenly the ball of yarn was blown across the deck toward Mandie and Celia.

"Oh, goodness!" Mandie said. She held on to Snowball's leash and hurried after the yarn as it unwound in front of them.

The young woman stood up and watched as she held on to the piece she had knitted.

"Watch out!" Celia yelled above the roar of the wind as Snowball turned in front of Mandie to run after the ball of yarn. But her warning was not quick enough, and Mandie stumbled over the white kitten, and slipped to the floor with a hard thump. Snowball, free from restraint, raced away down the deck, his red leash trailing behind him.

"Oh, Snowball!" Mandie exclaimed, trying to untangle her long skirts so she could get up and go after him.

Celia offered her hand and asked, "Are you all right, Mandie?"

Mandie struggled to her feet and shook out her rumpled skirts. "I'm all right but Snowball got away," she said with a loud sigh.

The young woman came to her side and asked, "All right, *ja*?" Mandie immediately recognized the accent as German, and knew that *ja* meant yes.

"*Ja*," Mandie said with a smile. "I'm all right. Now I have to go find my cat." She noticed that the girl was pretty, with sandy-colored hair and blue-gray eyes.

"So sorry," the girl said. She rapidly wound up the loose yarn. "I help find cat." She quickly bundled the yarn into a bag she was carrying and followed the girls down the deck.

Mandie hurried along, watching for Snowball. Celia and the young woman followed. Mandie finally spotted him. His leash had caught on a hook by the rail and he was pawing with all his might trying to get loose.

"Ah-ha!" Mandie said, bending to free the leash. "You caught yourself this time." She straightened out the leash and wrapped the end around her wrist. "You won't be getting away from me again."

The young woman and Celia watched. "I am glad that you have caught the cat," the stranger said.

"So am I," Mandie said with a little laugh. "Snowball runs away every chance he gets."

"*Ja*, I know that thing, too," the young woman said, and then she asked, "You do not remember me, *nein*?"

Mandie knew *nein* was German for "no." She quickly scrutinized the woman's face, and Celia did likewise. She didn't remember ever seeing the young woman before.

"No, I'm sorry, but I don't remember you," Mandie said, still trying to figure out who the young woman was.

"At the castle of the Baroness Geissler I came to dinner," the girl explained. "I am cousin of Rupert. I go to New York now to visit Rupert's mother."

"Oh, yes, we stayed at the castle. But the baroness

had so many guests. I'm sorry, I don't remember you," Mandie apologized. "My name is Mandie Shaw and this is my friend, Celia Hamilton."

"*Ja,* I know," the girl said, smiling. "My name is Mary Kurtz. And how is your grandmother?"

"Oh, Grandmother . . . she's all right, I suppose . . . just a little tired, and she needs some rest," Mandie told her. A sudden gust of wind almost displaced her bonnet as she reached to hold on to it. "I think we have to go inside now. It's too windy out here. We'll probably see you later."

"*Ja,* I must go, too," Mary said, waving to them as she hurried toward the nearest door.

Mandie and Celia walked back along the deck toward the doorway they had come through. Mandie picked up Snowball and carried him since he refused to walk at the end of his leash.

"I don't remember her, do you?" Mandie asked.

"No, I don't," Celia said. "I know there were a lot of people coming and going at the castle while we were there, but I think I would remember anyone I saw."

"Especially anyone kin to Rupert, of all people," Mandie added. She pushed open the door and Celia followed her inside. Snowball was content again to walk at the end of his leash.

"And she said she was going to visit Rupert's mother in New York," Celia remarked. "She must not be on friendly terms with Rupert, because you know how Rupert feels about his mother marrying that American."

"I know and—" Mandie stopped to listen. She could hear a baby crying somewhere nearby and it reminded her of her little brother, Samuel, back home. She looked around and then said, "Let's see where that baby is."

When they turned the corner of the corridor, Mandie spotted a young woman standing in a small alcove, and holding a crying baby. She rushed forward and asked above the cries, "Is the baby sick?"

The young woman looked at her and then at Celia and finally replied, "No, I think it's the excitement of being on the ship." She cuddled the baby closer.

"Could I hold him?" Mandie asked, giving the end of Snowball's leash to Celia, and then wondering why in the world she'd asked such a question. She didn't really care for crying babies. Her little brother had never seemed to stop crying when she was home from school.

The young woman looked at Mandie for a moment and then held the baby out to her. The instant Mandie took the child, it stopped crying and looked at her with solemn blue eyes.

"He's stopped crying now," Mandie said, hastily offering the baby back to the woman.

"Yes, he has," the woman said, but as she took the baby, he began screaming again.

"We have to go now," Mandie said quickly, above the baby's crying. She snatched the end of Snowball's leash from Celia and practically ran down the corridor.

Celia caught up with her and anxiously asked, "What's wrong, Mandie?"

Mandie turned to look at her friend and said, "Nothing, nothing." She stopped walking. "I suppose the crying baby brought back bad memories about the way I acted when my little brother was born."

Celia looked at her and said, "I understand, but—"

"We're going home now," Mandie interrupted, "and I will never act that way again. Come on. It's probably time to eat." She hurried on down the corridor and Celia rushed to keep up with her.

They were both walking so fast when they reached an intersection in the corridor that Celia almost fell on top of Mandie as she stopped to stare ahead.

Coming directly toward them was the strange woman

they had first encountered on the ship going to Europe—
Miss Lucretia Wham!

Mandie and Celia looked at each other in surprise. The
woman saw them and continued coming toward them.

"Don't worry, dears, I'm not working this time. I am
on my way home, just as you two are," Miss Wham told
them. She was wearing the same expensive-looking black
clothes that didn't seem to fit, with that enormous dia-
mond brooch at her throat. Diamonds sparkled from gold
rings on her bony fingers as she clutched her purse.

"Yes, ma'am," Mandie said. "It's time for everybody
to go home." She wasn't too anxious to talk to the woman
after all she and Celia and Jonathan had been through
in Europe because of her. "But right now I think it's time
for us to go eat."

"Yes, that's where we were headed," Celia agreed.

"Of course, dears. See you later," Miss Wham said
and continued on her way in the opposite direction.

As soon as the woman was out of hearing, Mandie
moaned loudly and said, "Of all people to be on this ship!"

"But she said she's not working, Mandie. She won't
be bothering us," Celia said.

"I'm not so sure about that," Mandie said as they went
to look for Molly and Uncle Ned, and to find out if Mrs.
Taft was ready to eat.

But then, the ship was awfully big. Maybe they
wouldn't see Miss Wham again.

Chapter 3 / "Where Is My Mother?"

Mrs. Taft turned out to be good at predicting the weather. Heavy rains and high winds accompanied Mandie and her friends all the way across the ocean to the dock in Charleston, South Carolina.

Neither Miss Wham nor Mary Kurtz was seen by the girls again, probably because most of the ship's passengers stayed in their cabins, unable to cope with the stormy waters. Mandie and Celia spent their time catching up on their journals, reading, and teaching Molly table tennis in the game rooms.

Mrs. Taft quickly directed the girls' packing in preparation for disembarking. "Please be sure y'all find all your belongings and Molly's, too, and put them inside the trunks. We don't need to be bothered with loose baggage, because we're taking the train straight to Franklin, North Carolina, when we get off this boat," she told the girls as everyone hurried around collecting clothes and belongings.

Mandie stopped to look at her grandmother. "Are we not going to see the Pattons while we're in Charleston?" she asked. The Pattons were old friends of Mandie's mother and grandmother.

"No, dear, the train schedule won't permit it," Mrs. Taft told her. "And Senator Morton is getting the train going in the opposite direction to his home. Now, we have to be ready to leave as soon as we dock, so get everything ready for the stewards to take ashore."

"Yes, Grandmother," Mandie said, continuing with her packing. She had been secretly hoping she would have a chance to see Tommy Patton in Charleston. But school would be starting soon, and he'd be back in Asheville at Mr. Chadwick's School for Boys, which was near Misses Heathwoods' School for Girls that she and Celia attended.

Celia closed the lid on her trunk and then sat on it to try to force it shut. "I don't know why everything won't fit back in the way it was when we left home," she mumbled.

"That's because we bought a lot of things," Mandie reminded her. "Scarves and bracelets, and those wooden Dutch shoes, and—"

"But what I bought isn't very big and doesn't take up much room," Celia complained.

Mandie came to help Celia fasten the trunk. She immediately spotted the corner of a book sticking out from under the end of the lid. "There!" she said, pointing to it. "You need to open the lid and push that book inside."

Celia stood up and looked. "Well, no wonder it wouldn't close right," she said, quickly raising the lid and shoving the book inside. Then she was able to shut and lock it. After she was done, she went to look out the porthole.

Mandie glanced at her friend. Celia seemed to be absentminded, as though she had something on her mind.

Mandie had also noticed that Celia hadn't eaten much breakfast and had seemed to be lost in thought.

Mrs. Taft came back into the room. "If you girls are finished, let's get our bonnets and go out to the rail so we can be some of the first off the ship," she said, glancing around. "Uncle Ned and Senator Morton are to meet us there with Molly. Ready?"

"Yes, Grandmother," Mandie said, hastily tying on her bonnet as she passed the mirror on the wall, and then picking up her purse and Snowball. Celia took time to tuck in the loose ends of her hair as she put on her bonnet.

As Mrs. Taft and the girls hurried down the corridor, Mandie noticed that her grandmother's pep seemed to have been restored. The girls had to take big steps to keep up with her. Most of the days crossing the ocean Mrs. Taft had spent in her room, but now she was evidently revitalized with the prospect of going ashore.

Senator Morton was able to rent a waiting hack, which rushed them to the depot just in time to board the train. Mandie realized then that her grandmother had been right about the schedule. The only way they could have stopped to visit the Pattons would have been to stay over in Charleston until the next train went to North Carolina, and that could have been several days.

"I'm glad we didn't stop to see the Pattons, Grandmother," Mandie said, as she and Celia, with Molly between them, sat in front of Mrs. Taft and Senator Taft on the end seats, which could be flipped to face forward or backward. Uncle Ned had gone into another car where he had seen friends on the train. "It would have just delayed us getting home."

Mrs. Taft looked at her and said, "That's why we didn't let the Pattons know we were coming through Charleston.

I'm in a hurry to end this long journey, and I know everyone else must be too."

"Yes, and I'm sorry I'll have to get off up the track a ways to change trains," Senator Morton told her. "But you understand I must get home before going back to Washington."

"Of course," Mrs. Taft replied.

"But you will come to see us sometime, won't you, Senator Morton?" Mandie asked. She held tightly to Snowball's leash as he walked around her ankles.

"At the very first opportunity I will be knocking on your door, young lady," the senator said with a smile. "This has been a most enjoyable journey with you young people, and also with your grandmother, of course."

"I don't know what we would have done without you," Mrs. Taft told him. She smiled as she looked into his face.

"I'm sure you could have managed very well without me along. However, I'm glad you feel that way," the senator said as he smiled back at her.

Mandie watched the two older people. *I wonder if they are in love?* she pondered. *Do people in love act that way? There is certainly some attraction between them, but then the senator knew my grandfather long ago. Maybe he's just being nice to his friend's widow.*

The conductor could be heard over the roar of the train, "All aboard, last call! Last call! All aboard!" And the train jerked and bumped and suddenly jumped forward up the railroad tracks.

Molly was exhausted from the long journey and nodded in her seat. Mandie and Celia moved her into the seat next to the window, got a pillow from the conductor, and made her comfortable.

The two girls walked up and down the aisles with Snowball in tow as the train lurched around curves, puffed up hills, and flew on downgrades.

"This is good exercise," Mandie said, laughing as she held on to the handle on the back of a seat on the aisle. Snowball managed to clutch the carpet with his claws to keep from being thrown around when the train went around bends.

"After all that turbulence on the ship you'd think we'd be able to stand up on this train, but I believe this is worse than the ship," Celia said, smiling as she grasped her long skirts and firmly planted her feet.

"I don't mind it too much because I know every jerk, rumble, and roar carries us nearer home," Mandie said. "I'm glad you're coming home with me before you go on to your home, Celia." The girls walked on down the aisle.

Celia hesitated a moment, glanced at Mandie, and said, "But I'm not going home with you, Mandie. My aunt Rebecca is supposed to meet us at the depot in Franklin and take me on home. You see, I'd have to get this same train to leave Franklin later."

Mandie stopped and stared at Celia as she asked, "Why didn't anyone tell me this? I didn't know you weren't coming to my house."

"I suppose your grandmother had Uncle Ned send a message to my aunt before we left England," Celia explained. "Anyway, I didn't know either until we were ready to dock in Charleston. Then your grandmother told me Aunt Rebecca would be meeting me at the depot in North Carolina."

Mandie frowned. She remembered the morning when Uncle Ned had been late for breakfast and there had been some silent communication between him and Mrs. Taft. But then why was this kept secret from her?

Celia touched her arm and said, "But I'll see you at school, Mandie, and that's not long off."

Mandie straightened her shoulders, looked at Celia, and said, "Oh, well, I suppose Molly and I will be going home with Grandmother to Asheville when school starts."

"No, Mandie, Molly is going with me," Celia said.

The two girls stopped and looked at each other. "Didn't you know that either, Mandie?"

"Well, why is Molly going home with you? I thought my grandmother had custody of her until we find her aunt," Mandie said, frowning again.

"I think the last time her aunt was heard from she was living in Virginia, and I suppose since I live in Virginia it would be more convenient to have Molly there until we locate her aunt," Celia said.

"You knew all these things, Celia, and didn't bother to tell me?" Mandie questioned her friend. "Why hasn't anyone told me anything?"

"I'm sorry, Mandie, but I thought your grandmother would tell you, because it's her business, you know. Please don't be angry with me," Celia said, again reaching to touch Mandie's arm as they stood there in the middle of the aisle.

"I'm not angry with you, Celia. I never could get mad at you," Mandie replied. "I just don't understand why Grandmother has quit talking to me about things that involve me. She has gotten so secretive." Mandie looked down through the car and saw her grandmother resting with her eyes closed.

"Well, anyway, now you know what the plans are," Celia said, moving forward. "Let's go sit a while and watch the scenery go by."

The girls returned to their seats. Mandie stared out the window at the passing landscape but her thoughts were not on it. She was worried about her relationship with her grandmother. Was Mrs. Taft angry with her about something? Why had she told Celia all this and not Mandie? After all, Celia was just a friend, but Mandie was Mrs. Taft's granddaughter.

Uncle Ned never did return to their car until he and Senator Morton got off at a stop along the way. Then he waved at Mandie and said, "Papoose, be good. See you at home."

"I will, Uncle Ned," Mandie replied, waving back as he left the car. She noticed Senator Morton and her grandmother looking sadly at each other as they said goodbye. Evidently they hated parting.

Mrs. Taft closed her eyes and seemed to be sleeping most of the rest of the way. Molly was sleepyheaded, too. When they arrived at the depot in Franklin, Molly finally yawned, stretched, and stood up after Mandie shook her awake.

Mandie, overjoyed at being home again, watched out the window as the train slowed down and then came to a bumping halt.

"I see your aunt Rebecca out there on the platform," Mandie told Celia as the girls reached for their things in the rack overhead. "And I believe that's—yes, it is—Mr. Jason has come to take us home!"

"You're right," Celia agreed as she bent to look out the window.

Mrs. Taft stood up and told Celia, "You just stay right here, dear. Your aunt Rebecca will be getting on and I'm sure she has the necessary tickets for you both."

Mandie glanced at her grandmother, who was moving forward toward the door of the train car. Mrs. Taft looked back and saw Molly following her. She stopped and said to the child, "Molly, you stay here with Celia. You're going home with her on this train."

"But I got you for me grandmother now," Molly complained as she looked up at Mrs. Taft.

Mrs. Taft smiled and stooped to give the child a hug. "I'll still be your grandmother if you like, but right now Celia and her aunt Rebecca are taking you home with them. I promise to see you sometime real soon."

Molly shrugged and without a word turned back to Celia, who gave her a squeeze as she put her back up on the seat. Then Celia reached to put her arms around Mandie.

Mandie hugged her back, and as she leaned back to tell Celia goodbye she was sure she saw tears in Celia's green eyes. "Hey, you don't have to cry about it. We'll be seeing each other real soon at school," Mandie said with a slight laugh.

Celia quickly blinked her eyes and looked away from Mandie's stare. "Oh, I'm not crying, Mandie." she said, and she turned quickly to sit down next to Molly. Without glancing up, she said, "See you at school, Mandie."

Mandie, anxious to get off the train, waved back at her and followed her grandmother outside. She then waved to Celia's aunt Rebecca who was just boarding.

Jason Bond, Mandie's uncle John's big, tall, gray-haired caretaker, was standing on the platform waiting. Mrs. Taft rushed ahead of Mandie, said something to him that Mandie could not hear, and when he replied, she almost stumbled down the steps of the platform in her haste to get to the waiting buggy. Mr. Bond looked back at Mandie as he helped Mrs. Taft, and Mandie followed.

By the time Mandie reached the vehicle, Mrs. Taft was already seated inside, and Jason Bond turned to assist Mandie with the small bag she was carrying. Mandie tiptoed to plant a kiss on the old man's cheek as she said excitedly, "Oh, Mr. Jason, I'm so glad to be home."

Without looking at her, the old man replied, "Yes, Missy, I'm glad you're back, too." As she stepped up beside Mrs. Taft, Jason Bond jumped up on the seat and said, "Now let's get this here vehicle home. Abraham will come back for your trunks."

Uncle John's house, where Mandie lived with him and her mother since their marriage, was really within walking distance of the train depot. However, Mandie knew they had to ride because of the small bags they were carrying. Otherwise she would have liked to walk along the streets and enjoy seeing everything along the way. Snowball didn't seem to like the fast ride, and he meowed in complaint as Mandie held him tight.

As they turned the corner of the street where Uncle John lived, Mandie was surprised to see buggies and other vehicles parked the length of it on both sides. Believing her grandmother to be angry with her about something, Mandie didn't remark aloud, but she thought to herself, *Goodness, all these people must have come to welcome us back home.*

Then when Mr. Bond brought the buggy to a halt in front of Uncle John's huge white house, Mandie saw the yard was full of people. She finally looked at her grandmother, who didn't seem to notice anything unusual.

"Grandmother, all these people—have they come to welcome us back home? Who are they?" Mandie asked as her grandmother was assisted down from the buggy by Mr. Bond.

"Yes, dear," Mrs. Taft replied as she rushed forward up the walkway, with Mr. Bond hurrying alongside her.

Mandie frowned as she stopped to look about the yard. She didn't see anyone she knew. Then as she stood there staring, she saw Joe Woodard, her lifelong friend, run toward her as fast as his long, gangly legs would carry him. She had gone to school with Joe at Charley Gap, where she had lived with her father before he died. Joe was the son of the family physician, Dr. Woodard.

"Mandie!" Joe cried in a shaky voice as he tightly embraced her.

Mandie had never seen him display such emotion before and was shocked at his behavior. She pushed back to look up into his young face. "Why, Joe, I've only been gone to Europe for a few weeks," she said with a little laugh, and then when Joe wouldn't look directly at her, she demanded, "Joe Woodard, something's wrong! What is it? Tell me!"

Joe, still not looking into her face, said, "That's not for me to say, Mandie." When Mandie suddenly pushed him away, he added, "I'm sorry, because I do love you."

Mandie raced as fast as her legs would carry her toward the front door of the house. Ignoring greetings along the way, she pushed people aside and ran inside. She collided with Liza, the young Negro maid who worked for Uncle John and who was a dear friend of Mandie's. She dropped Snowball to the floor and he went racing off.

"Oh, Missy 'Manda," Liza said with a loud moan as she put an arm around Mandie.

Mandie realized Liza was not her usual smiling, joking self. "What is it, Liza? Where is my mother? Where is my mother?" Mandie began frantically crying as she turned toward the parlor.

Liza grabbed her and held her tight. "She don't be in there, Missy 'Manda," Liza said. "She be in huh bedroom up de stairs."

Mandie pulled away and said, "In her bedroom?" Then she realized she didn't know where Mrs. Taft had gone. "Did my grandmother go up there?"

"Dat she did," Liza said. "But, Missy, you cain't go in huh room."

Mandie felt as though her heart would jump out of her chest, and as though she were in a cloud. "Why can't I?" she asked as she pulled away from Liza and raced toward the steps.

Liza ran after Mandie and tried to persuade her not to go up the steps, but Mandie fiercely fought her and finally reached the top of the stairs. The upstairs hallway was filled with people sitting in chairs along the walls as she sped toward her mother's bedroom.

"Papoose!" Uncle Ned's voice came to her as she paused to look back. He was striding toward her with open arms, and before she could continue he embraced her, and Morning Star, his wife, joined him.

He had ridden a horse after leaving the train. By taking shortcuts through woods and country, he had arrived before Mandie's train.

"Uncle Ned, what is it? I want to see my mother! My mother!" Mandie frantically pushed at him but was unable to extricate herself from his arms.

Uncle Ned picked her up and hurried down the hallway to a window seat away from the other people. He sat down and held Mandie in his lap while she kicked and squirmed to free herself.

"Papoose, Mother not want Papoose come to her room," Uncle Ned tried to tell her.

Mandie paused long enough to ask, "Why does my mother not want me to come to her room? Why?"

"Mother of Papoose sick," Uncle Ned began, and this brought a fresh effort on Mandie's part to break away from him, but he held her tight.

"Uncle Ned, I want to see my mother!" she cried. "I want my mother!"

"Papoose must listen." Uncle Ned finally shook her and Mandie hushed. "Mother of Papoose sick. Fever. Papoose catch if go in her room. Papoose see mother when she get better."

Mandie gasped and almost collapsed. "My mother has the fever? Nobody told me. Nobody told me!" she cried. Then she began fighting again. "I am going to see my mother."

"Uncle John say for Papoose to stay out of mother's room. He stay with mother while sick," Uncle Ned tried to explain. "He already have fever. He won't get it again. He stay with mother of Papoose. Does not want Papoose to get it, too."

Mandie calmed down enough to listen. "Oh, dear God, please don't take my mother away from me, too. You already have my father," she cried aloud as Uncle Ned tried to smooth her ruffled hair. Her bonnet had fallen back on her shoulders.

"Yes, dear God, you will make mother of Papoose well we trust," Uncle Ned added as he held Mandie tightly in his arms.

Mandie finally relaxed in the old Indian's arms. She didn't have any strength left to fight her way free.

"All we can do is trust Big God to make mother of Papoose well again," Uncle Ned said softly to her.

Mandie, shaking with sobs, looked up at Uncle Ned and asked, "Where is Dr. Woodard? Is he here? Can't he make my mother well again? Can't he?"

"Doctor here every day, every night. All these people pray," Uncle Ned told her.

"Uncle Ned, I'm afraid. I'm afraid my mother will—go away and leave me," Mandie sobbed on his shoulder.

"Then Papoose say verse, remember?" Uncle Ned reminded her.

Mandie leaned back to look into his face and said, "Say it with me, Uncle Ned." She reached for his wrinkled old hand and together they repeated Mandie's favorite Bible verse, " 'What time I am afraid I will put my trust in Thee.' Oh, dear God, I mean it with all my heart," Mandie added.

Whenever Mandie was afraid for any reason at all, the verse comforted her as she realized God was powerful to help her. She kissed Uncle Ned on the cheek and said, "I'd better go to my room now, Uncle Ned, and get cleaned up." She stood up, shook out her long skirts, and with a trembling voice said, "That was really a dirty train ride."

Uncle Ned smiled at her and said, "Go to room, Papoose. I keep watch. I see Papoose later."

Mandie hugged Morning Star, who had been sitting there all the time, then she turned to hurry to her room. She would clean up, change clothes, and then she would come back down the hallway to check on her mother.

Chapter 4 / Visitor in the Night

When Mandie turned the bend in the corridor toward her room, she was relieved to see through her tear-filled eyes that there were no people in this hallway. She had her hand on the knob ready to open the door when a woman's voice nearby said, "So you are Amanda." Mandie quickly entered her room without looking around and closed the door. She was in no condition to talk to anyone. And she had no idea who the woman was or where she had appeared from. She was sure there had been no one there when she entered the hallway.

Mumbling to herself, "Oh, Mother, I love you. Please get well." Mandie dabbed at her eyes with her handkerchief. She was so proud of her blue and gold room, but this time there was no joy in entering it. Without a glance around she hastily pulled off her traveling suit, poured water into the bowl from the pitcher on the washstand, and freshened up. She pulled down the first dress she touched in the chifferobe and quickly put it on. In her haste she mismatched the buttons on the waist of the blue gingham dress and didn't even notice it.

"Dear Lord, please let this all be just a bad dream, please," she begged as she brushed out her long blonde hair and re-braided it.

She felt as though she were in a daze. Even her vision was out of focus through the tears in her blue eyes. But somehow she was going to get to her mother. She didn't care about the fever, or about what other people were doing to prevent her from entering her mother's room. She had to see her mother. She had to be sure she was still there.

Just as Mandie was ready to leave her room, she heard voices outside the door.

"Lawsy mercy, Missy, what you be doin' in dis heah house of fever?" Liza was exclaiming. "Now you jes' run right home and don't you be comin' back. You knows bettuh than comin' in this house. Now git!"

Polly Cornwallis, Mandie's friend next door, replied, "But, Liza, Mandie doesn't have the fever. I just want to talk to her a minute."

"No, no, no!" Liza scolded. "Now you git back home where you belong."

"Oh, please, Liza," Polly begged. "Couldn't I just see her for a minute? After all, she's been gone all this time to Europe, and I'd like to speak to her for just a minute. Please."

"I says no, Missy, and I means no," Liza said firmly. "I'm sure Missy 'Manda ain't int'rested in talkin' to you 'bout Europe when huh mother's lyin' in there 'bout to leave dis world. Now you gwine leave or do I has to call fo' help to throw you out? And I will, believe me."

"All right, I'll go home—this time," Polly finally said with a loud sigh. "But I'll catch Mandie later."

"Now git!" Liza told her, loudly clapping her hands at the girl.

"I'm going," Polly said, as Mandie heard her hurrying down the hallway.

Mandie listened to hear whether Liza was still in the hallway, but she couldn't hear a sound. She decided to open the door far enough to look outside. As she did, she came face-to-face with Liza, who was turning to sit on a chair in the hallway.

"Liza, what are you doing here? Don't you have to help downstairs with all those people?" Mandie asked in a voice husky from crying.

"Missy 'Manda, you be de most impor'ant thing to me right now, and I plans to sit right heah and see you ain't disturbed," Liza said with a solemn face. Her usual happy, carefree ways seemed to have left her.

Mandie tried to think up some way to get her to leave. She knew Liza would follow her anywhere she went in the house to prevent her from going near her mother's bedroom where the fever raged.

"You don't have to stay here, because I think I'll just lie down and rest awhile," Mandie told her. "And I just won't answer if anyone knocks on my door."

"Missy 'Manda, I been knowin' you long 'nuff to know you ain't gwine sit in dat room and not answer de door," Liza told her. "So I jes' stay right heah."

Mandie was too tired to argue, and she couldn't think up any way to get Liza to leave.

"All right, waste your time then, Liza, but I'm going to lie down," Mandie told her and closed the door.

Mandie lay down across the silky bedspread. She buried her face in her hands. Somehow she would get out of this room . . . somehow.

Before long Mandie heard another voice outside her

door. This time it was her friend Joe Woodard.

"Why, Liza, what are you doing sitting here in the hall?" Joe asked.

"Might as well go on back downstairs, doctuh son," Liza told Joe. "You ain't gwine 'sturb Missy 'Manda. She be restin'."

"I only wanted to speak to her a minute," Joe argued.

"Now you knows well as I does decent boys don't go callin' on young ladies in their bedroom. So you jes' have to wait, like ever'body else," Liza said.

"But, Liza, I wasn't going into her bedroom. I only wanted to speak to her at the door. I promise I won't go inside," Joe insisted.

"Well, you ain't gwine speak to huh long as I sits out heah and I ain't got no plans to leave," Liza replied. "Now you jes' git."

"All right, all right, I won't argue with you," Joe said. "But I'll catch Mandie as soon as she comes out of her room and I'll be watching for her."

"Well, you ain't watchin' up heah. You git back downstairs, you heah?" Liza said loudly.

"I'm going," Joe called back as Mandie heard him walking away.

Now what did Joe want to say to me? Mandie thought. *Looks like all those people would leave me alone. I don't want to talk to anyone. All I want right now is to get out of this room without Liza seeing me.*

Mandie suddenly sat up on the bed. She had an idea that might work. She stood up and went to open the door just a crack. Liza was still there and immediately saw Mandie.

"Liza, I'm hungry. It's been a long time since we ate," Mandie began. "Do you think you could get something?"

Liza quickly stood up to look at Mandie as she said,

"Lawsy mercy, Missy 'Manda, I'se sorry, but I plumb fo'got 'bout food. What you want?"

Mandie, relieved that Liza was cooperating with her scheme, said, "Whatever you have downstairs. Just anything."

"It don't be long till mealtime," Liza said. "Supposin' I jes' bring you a glass of tea and some cookies? That 'nuff fo' now?"

"Sure, Liza, and you could make that milk instead of tea, if you don't mind," Mandie said with a sigh.

"Oh, but, Missy 'Manda, I cain't bring you milk," Liza said. "They be sayin' milk carries germs if it gits 'round de fever, so everybody dey been drinkin' tea."

"That's all right, Liza. Tea will be fine," Mandie said as the young Negro girl turned to leave. "Thank you."

"I be right back, Missy 'Manda," Liza called back to her. "You stay in yo' room, you hears?"

Mandie didn't answer, but waited until Liza had turned the corner of the hallway before she stepped out of her room and closed the door. Her mother's bedroom was in another wing of the house, and she was hoping she wouldn't have to walk past any of the visitors on her way. She carefully peeked around the corner as she came to the intersection in the hall where she would have to go left.

"No one in sight! Thank goodness!" Mandie said to herself.

She slowly moved on and finally came to the wing where her mother's bedroom was. Still not seeing anyone in the hallway, she rushed forward to the closed door of her mother's room. She listened but couldn't hear a sound inside.

Oh, Mother, please be in there! Mandie cried silently.

She gave the door a hard push and it swung open.

She caught a glimpse of other people in the room, but her eyes focused on her mother in the big bed. Before anyone could stop her, she ran forward and was about to fall down beside the bed when strong hands grabbed her and held her tight. She looked up into the face of Uncle John.

"My mother! Uncle John, I want to see my mother!" she cried as she tried to break loose.

"No, Amanda, darling, you can't touch your mother. The fever is highly contagious, and you are not supposed to be in this room at all," Uncle John told her as he held her tight.

"But, Uncle John, is my mother going to get well?" Mandie practically screamed.

Dr. Woodard spoke from beside the bed, "Now, Miss Amanda, you must go back to your room and not come in here again. We don't want you to get sick, too."

"I want to see my mother!" Mandie was trying to push Uncle John's arms away when another set of strong arms pulled her from behind.

"Y'all jes' let my chile be now," Aunt Lou, Uncle John's big Negro housekeeper, said loudly. "She jes' wants to look at huh mother and dat she gwine do and den we'll take huh to huh room."

"All right, but look only," Uncle John agreed.

Mandie swung around to hug the huge woman. "Oh, Aunt Lou, I've missed you so much," she told her. "I only want to be sure my mother is still here." Her voice trembled with every word.

Aunt Lou held Mandie tight as she turned her around to look at her mother in the big bed.

"Oh, Mother, I love you!" Mandie cried from across the room where Aunt Lou held her. Her mother looked so thin and worn out lying there. Her eyes were closed and she began moaning and tossing about, as though she'd heard Mandie's cry.

Mandie turned to Dr. Woodard and asked, "Is—is my mother—going to—get well? Is she? Tell me!" She sobbed loudly.

"We're doing all we know how to do, Miss Amanda. All we can do is just hope and pray. And remember, young lady, prayer can change things," Dr. Woodard replied.

"I can't lose my mother! I can't!" Mandie began crying, and tears blinded her as Uncle John picked her up and took her out into the hallway. There they met up with Liza.

"Get her back to her room and give her a strong bath at once, Liza. Change all her clothes, too," Uncle John told the Negro girl.

"Yessuh, I do dat," Liza said, putting an arm around Mandie and leading her down the hallway. Uncle John went back into the sickroom. "Missy 'Manda, how come you lies to me and leaves yo' room like dat? I only tryin' to take care of you fo' yo' own good."

Mandie tried to talk but she could only sob. She had been stunned by the sight of her mother. She'd looked so helpless and thin lying on that big bed.

Once inside her room, Mandie didn't protest when Liza quickly undressed her and gave her a bath as Uncle John had instructed. The room seemed to float around as Mandie struggled into clean clothes with the maid's help.

"Now you drinks some of dis heah tea and rest," Liza told her. She held out the glass of tea she had brought from the kitchen.

Mandie managed to swallow half of it before she collapsed on the bed. Liza had turned down the bedspread and now she gently pulled a cotton sheet over Mandie and tiptoed from the room. She once again took up her watch in the chair outside the door.

Mandie slept fitfully through the rest of the day and into the night. When she heard the clock strike three, she felt a presence in her room. She strained to open her eyes. A full moon was hanging outside her window. Snowball was on the foot of her bed. He uttered a low growl, his fur ruffled up, and he crept up to Mandie's pillow.

Mandie raised up on her elbow. Suddenly a vision seemed to hover over her bed. A golden light surrounded it and illuminated the room. Mandie felt frozen in time. She could only stare.

As she watched the vision seemed to form into a beautiful young person. As it spoke to her, Mandie felt warmed and comforted.

"Peace," the musical voice said softly. "You will know. You will know."

When Mandie opened her mouth to ask, "Know what?" the vision suddenly evaporated.

The brilliant light was gone. Only the full moon allowed Mandie to see Snowball return to the foot of the bed and curl up. Mandie slipped into peaceful sleep until morning.

When Mandie woke the next day, she immediately sat up and rubbed her eyes. Had an angel appeared to her during the night? Or had she dreamed it?

"It had to be an angel," Mandie whispered breathlessly to herself. "I can still see the beautiful glowing vision." She paused to recollect what had happened. The angel had said, "Peace. You will know. You will know."

"And when I started to ask 'Know what?' it completely disappeared."

She slid off the high bed and walked around the room. Snowball sat up on the bed and washed his face.

Mandie turned to her cat suddenly and said, "You saw it, too. I remember how you acted—like you were frightened. You crawled up on my pillow."

Mandie paced about the room as she pondered the problem of what she was supposed to *know*.

Then there was a soft knock on her bedroom door and Liza stuck her head inside.

"I thought I heerd you up, Missy 'Manda," Liza said as she came on into the room. "And I'm glad to see you're feelin' better."

Mandie stopped to look at Liza and she realized she did feel better—much better—than she had since arriving home. But why? Why was she feeling better when her mother was so ill?

"Liza, how is my mother? Is she better this morning?" Mandie asked, quickly stepping closer to Liza.

"Missy 'Manda, I don't be knowin'," Liza said as she threw back the sheet and began straightening the rumpled bed. "But I'll find out fo' you." She gave the covers a last tug, then stood up to look at Mandie. "Now what you be wantin' fo' breakfus'?"

"Breakfast?" Mandie asked.

"It do be breakfus' time, Missy 'Manda," Liza explained. "After dat hot bath, you slept right through de evening and on through de night, and now it's mawnin' and time fo' breakfus'."

"I'll get dressed and go downstairs to eat," Mandie said, and then suddenly remembering all the strangers in the house, she changed her mind and said, "No, I won't either. If you'll bring me something up here, I'll eat it here. Just whatever Jenny has in the kitchen will do. I'm not much hungry."

Liza placed her hands on her hips and looked straight into Mandie's eyes as she asked, "Now, Missy 'Manda, you ain't plannin' to leave dis room agin whilst I'se gone, is you? Like you did yesta'day?"

Liza's question brought back the memory of seeing her sick mother and caused a deep pain in her chest. "I promise I'll get dressed and be right here when you come back," Mandie told her.

"I heah you. You'll be right heah when I come back, but where you gwine whilst I'm gone?" Liza insisted on knowing.

"Why, Liza, I'm not going anywhere," Mandie assured her. She hesitated a moment and added, "I don't want to see any of those people who are all over the house. I don't know them."

"Well, neithuh does I," Liza said. "From what I hears, some of 'em be kinpeople, de long-lost kind, where don't show up 'cept in times o' trouble." Then Liza surprised Mandie by reaching to put an arm around her as she said, "Now, Missy 'Manda, you does know I loves you. Dat's why I'se tryin' to take good care of you. We's done had too much sickness already widdout you agittin' de fever, too."

Before Mandie could say anything, Liza had quickly crossed the room and opened the door. "Now you stays right heah till I gits back wid de food," she said as she left the room, closing the door behind her.

Mandie loved Liza, too. They had been good friends ever since that first day when Mandie had come to live in her uncle John's house after her father died.

Suddenly Mandie realized she had endangered Liza's health, too. She had gone into the room where her mother had the fever and then Liza had to help her bathe. She was beginning to understand that the fever was very contagious and very dangerous.

And as she thought of her mother, Mandie remembered what had happened during the night. She pondered the angel's question. What would she know? The angel—and she firmly believed it must have been an angel—seemed to have a secret and had told Mandie she would know too. If she could only figure out what it was that she was supposed to know! What was the secret?

She couldn't remember whether the angel had said anything else. And what she could remember did not make any sense to her. But she realized she had felt a burden lift when the angel visited her.

When Liza came back with a tray of food and placed it on a table nearby, Mandie asked her to sit with her while she ate, sure that Liza had already had breakfast.

Mandie picked up her cup and drank some of the hot coffee. She watched Liza for a minute and then asked, "Liza, have you ever seen an angel?"

Liza's mouth flew open as she gasped and said, "Lawsy mercy, Missy 'Manda, what you be talkin' 'bout angels fo'?"

"I just wanted to know if you'd ever seen one," Mandie said, setting down her cup.

"No, and I don't wants to be seein' none eithuh," Liza told her.

"But, Liza, angels are nothing to be afraid of," Mandie said, and when Liza didn't answer right away, she asked, "Are they?"

"De only angel I ever heerd of is de angel of death, and we sho' don't want no angel of death in dis heah house," Liza said, getting up to walk around the room. "Now you git on wid dat breakfus'."

"But, Liza, I've heard people talk about a guardian angel," Mandie said. "That would be a good angel, wouldn't it, one that would watch over you?"

"Maybe, maybe not," Liza said quickly. "Now let's jes'

talk 'bout somethin' else, like what you plannin' on doin' today."

"What I'm planning on doing today," Mandie repeated as she bit into a hot roll. "I know there's something I'm supposed to know, but I don't know what it is."

"Missy 'Manda, you ain't quite makin' sense," Liza said. "Now I'se got things I has to do dis mawnin'. I cain't jes' sit heah and talk." She stood up.

"I'm sorry, Liza; you go ahead and do whatever you have to do. I'll stay here in my room for a while—*if* you'll go find out how my mother is and let me know first," Mandie told her.

"I do dat right now, Missy 'Manda," Liza said as she hurried toward the door. "Be right back. You wait now."

Mandie had only sipped at her coffee but had not touched a bite of food. Now she waited for Liza to return before continuing. And while she sat there she remembered saying her favorite Bible verse with Uncle Ned the day before, "What time I am afraid I will put my trust in Thee." And she knew that she would trust God to make her mother well again.

When Liza returned to the room Mandie anxiously looked at the girl's face. Liza didn't seem sad or happy, but when she spoke she had a slight smile as she said, "Dr. Woodard, he say she ain't no bettuh, but she ain't no worser eithuh, so dat means she be holdin' on tight. And he say he doin' all he know how."

Mandie thought that over for a moment and finally she said, "You're right about that. She's not any worse, so we can feel some hope, can't we?"

"Dat's right, Missy 'Manda," Liza said, looking down at the tray. "Now you kin git on wid dat breakfus' and I'll be back aftuh a while."

Mandie picked up the roll and nibbled on it as she said, "Thank you, Liza."

But when Liza again left the room, Mandie managed to eat only the roll and drink the coffee as she walked about the room trying to figure out what had really happened the night before. She was sure the angel had given her a message, but evidently she was too thick-headed to figure it all out.

Snowball's loud meow brought her out of her thoughts and she realized he had not been fed. She quickly placed the bacon from her plate on a saucer and set it under the table for him. He rushed at it with a hungry growl.

Then Mandie remembered the way her cat had acted when the angel appeared, and she wondered whether he had been afraid of it. She was frightened speechless herself until the angel spoke.

"You will know. You will know," the angel had said. *Know what?* Suddenly, Mandie gasped and stopped in her tracks.

"I do know, I do know!" she said. The angel was right. She scrambled around the room in search of her clothes. She understood the message now and she must not waste another minute.

She dressed quickly, then went to the desk near the window and opened the drawer. Shoving things around inside, she took out a small black book and laid it on the bed.

Chapter 5 / Sneaking Out

As she hastily put on a gingham dress, Mandie glanced out the window. She realized for the first time that it was drizzling rain outside.

"That's good. I can wear my cape with the hood and maybe no one will see me leave the house," Mandie said to herself as she grabbed the dark garment from its hanger in the chifferobe and put it on. "This may be a little warm but that's all right. As long as it keeps anyone from knowing who I am." She put the little black book in her pocket.

Snowball watched her from his perch on the dresser. Mandie cautiously opened the door to the hall and her cat quickly left the room and disappeared down the corridor. She stood there a moment, trying to decide what the easiest way out of the house would be.

"I don't want anyone to know what I'm doing," Mandie murmured to herself as she glanced up and down the hallway. "All those people are probably in the front hallway, so I'll just go down the back stairs."

Being careful not to make any noise and holding her breath most of the time, Mandie descended the back stairway, which was at the end of the corridor near her room.

As she reached the last step, she paused to listen. She could hear pots and pans being moved around in the kitchen nearby, but she didn't hear anybody talking.

"It's now or never," she whispered to herself. Tiptoeing the rest of the way, Mandie reached the outside door near the stairs and quickly slipped into the yard. This was a back entrance from the vegetable garden and was seldom used. Mandie realized she could have gone through the secret tunnel to leave the house, but she might have met up with someone before she got to its entrance. Anyway, this would be quicker and time was important.

She pulled the hood over her blonde head against the fine drizzle of rain, then rushed through the garden and into the road. She went all the way around the block to keep from walking in front of the house. Feeling that this was probably the most urgent thing she had ever done in her life, Mandie practically ran the rest of the way to the telegraph office by the depot.

Very few people were around and Mandie didn't see anyone she knew. The man behind the window smiled at her as he said, "Good morning, miss."

"Oh, good morning," Mandie said as she tugged the small black book out of her pocket. "I need to send an urgent message. I have the address in here." She quickly flipped through the pages of the little book.

"You must write the message on the pad here, miss," the man told her, pushing a pad of paper toward her.

"Oh, of course," Mandie said as she quickly took the pad and picked up a pencil. She tried to think what to say. Now that she was finally here at the telegraph office, she wasn't sure what to write in the message. Finally she began scribbling on the pad of paper.

To Dr. Samuel Hezekiah Plumbley,

She said the name to herself as she copied his New York address from her little book.

Please come quickly. My mother needs you bad. She is desperately ill with the fever. Dr. Woodard has done all he can. Please help us. Mandie Shaw.

She glanced over what she had written and handed the paper to the clerk.

"Let's see. This will cost—" the man began as he looked at the message.

Mandie quickly interrupted with a loud sigh, "Oh, I don't have any money with me. I didn't even think about money." Then she had a sudden idea as she added, "Please, mister, couldn't I just charge it right now, and then come back with the money later?"

The man looked at her, then glanced at the message. He said, "I see your name is Shaw, Mandie Shaw. Would you be any kin to Mr. John Shaw?"

"Yes, sir, he's my uncle. He married my mother, and my mother is terribly sick," Mandie replied. "Couldn't I come back later and pay for the message?"

"That won't be necessary, miss. Your uncle has an account here. I'll just put this on his bill," the clerk told her. "I'll get this out right away. And I'm sorry your mother is ill. Now don't worry about a thing. Just go on back home and I'll see that this Dr. Plumbley gets your message."

Mandie's face lit up with a big smile as she said,

"Thank you, thank you! I just know everything's going to be all right now."

As she left the telegraph office she felt like shouting. She was sure that this was what the angel had meant, that she would know how to help her mother. And if anyone could help her mother, it was Dr. Plumbley, who had lived in Franklin years before and who knew the Shaw family well. He had gone to New York to practice medicine and further his medical education. Mandie knew there must be more modern medical schools in New York than anywhere else. Surely Dr. Plumbley must have learned more modern ways to doctor than their old family friend and physician, Dr. Woodard, knew.

Pausing suddenly on the road, Mandie looked up at the sky as the rain wet her face. "Dear God, please let my mother live until Dr. Plumbley gets here. And please give Dr. Plumbley the knowledge to save my mother. Thank you, dear Lord."

She hurried on back to the house and was able to get to her room without seeing anyone. Inside her room, she removed the wet cape and hung it on a hook beside the chifferobe to dry. She unbraided and brushed out her damp hair. As she was re-braiding it she glanced out the window and saw that the drizzle had suddenly stopped and the sun was coming out.

Mandie walked over to the window to bask in the sunlight as she felt her burden lift. Looking down into the yard she saw someone creeping along behind the shrubbery and, as the person got closer, she realized it was her next door friend, Polly Cornwallis, whom Liza had run out of the house yesterday.

Polly happened to look up, and when she saw Mandie she began waving and making motions toward the back entrance door. Mandie understood that Polly was going to make another attempt to get to her room. And this time Liza was not around to stop her.

Mandie watched until Polly was out of sight around the house, and soon she heard a light tap on her door. She went to open it.

"Mandie, will you let me come in for a few minutes?" Polly asked, pushing back her long dark hair. Her eyes were as dark as chinquapins.

"Come on in, Polly," Mandie offered. "Sit down." Polly flopped in a big chair and Mandie sat on the bed.

"I'm sorry your mother is so ill, Mandie," Polly began. "But I just wanted to see you for a few minutes to get caught up with things. You were gone so long on your trip to Europe."

"We came back earlier than Grandmother had planned, and now I know why," Mandie said. "Evidently she knew my mother was sick with the fever. I don't know why she didn't let me know." She frowned as she thought about incidents unexplainable till now.

"She didn't let you know about your mother?" Polly asked with a little gasp. "Did she let you—" She stopped in midsentence and gave Mandie a sharp look.

Mandie looked at Polly and asked, "Well? Let me what?"

"Did she . . . What did she tell you when she decided to come home earlier than you were supposed to?" Polly asked in a rush of words.

"Nothing. She just said we were coming home. Why do you ask that?" Mandie said, frowning slightly as she looked at the girl.

"Where is your grandmother, Mandie? Did she stay here?" Polly asked.

Mandie realized she had not seen her grandmother since they had arrived. She didn't remember seeing her in the room with her mother. But then she was tired from the long journey and was probably resting in a room somewhere in the house.

"I'm sure she's around somewhere," Mandie replied. "And you know, Polly, you really shouldn't be in this house with the fever around."

"I've been in it before, like when your little brother got sick with the fever—" Polly began.

Mandie cut her short as she exclaimed, "My little brother! How could I have not even thought about him." She stood up. "He had the fever, too?"

Polly nodded in the affirmative.

"Is he all right? I haven't even seen him. I need to go find him, Polly," Mandie said, growing excited. She started toward the door.

Polly stood up and ran to stop Mandie from leaving the room. She stood between Mandie and the door. "Wait, Mandie. Wait," she said.

Mandie tried to step around her as she said, "What's wrong with you, Polly? I've got to find Samuel. With Mother sick and all, I need to look after him."

"Mandie!" Polly leaned toward Mandie and spoke loudly. "Listen to me!"

Mandie immediately stopped and stared at Polly. She felt her heart racing as she asked, "What is it, Polly? Tell me!"

Polly stared back at Mandie as they stood there facing each other. "He's ... not here ..." she began, and then stopped.

"Not here? Then where is he?" Mandie demanded, fear stabbing her heart.

"Mandie, he ... didn't ... survive," Polly finally explained.

Mandie collapsed onto the floor. "That can't be," she

cried, beating the carpet with her fists. "He can't be gone! He can't!" She suddenly stood up and looked at Polly again. "I don't believe you, Polly Cornwallis. I'm going to find my little brother!" She started for the door again.

Polly leaned against the door. "Mandie, he's not here. I know. That's the reason y'all came home. Your uncle John wired your grandmother that Samuel had died. Your mother got sick while y'all were on the way home," she tried to explain.

Mandie asked with a tremor in her voice, "Why has no one told me anything? Everybody else knew everything—Celia must have known, and Jonathan, and even when I get home nobody tells me anything. Why do they do this to me?"

"I'm sorry, Mandie," Polly said.

Mandie felt as if she were choking, and it was hard for her to speak. "Where ... where ... did they ..."

"Come on, Mandie, I'll show you," Polly offered. "He's buried in the graveyard across the road. I'll show you his grave. Come on."

Mandie, in a fog of grief, allowed Polly to take her hand, lead her down the back stairs, and around the house to the road. She followed Polly on into the cemetery until the girl stopped.

"Here, Mandie. This is his grave," Polly said, pointing to the fresh mound of dirt.

Mandie fell onto her knees to look at the inscription on the new tombstone: "Samuel Hezekiah Shaw ..." That was as far as her eyes read before tears blurred her vision. "Samuel! Samuel!" she cried. "I really did love you. I did! I did!"

Polly grasped Mandie's arm and tried to pull her to her feet. "Come on, Mandie, let's go back to your house," she told her.

Mandie pulled away from Polly and started screaming, "Oh, God, why have you taken my little brother? Why?" She buried her face in her hands. Guilt riddled her mind. She had not wanted a baby brother or sister when Samuel was born. She had done terrible things because of it, and now she thought God was punishing her. "I told you a long time ago I was sorry, God," she screamed as she raised her head. "Why did you do this to me?"

Mandie felt strong arms lift her from the ground and carry her away. She tried to fight but soon gave up. Her little brother was gone forever. There was no way she could bring him back.

She was taken back to her room and laid on her bed. She heard a man demand, "Get Liza. Now!" Mandie recognized the voice as Uncle Ned's. He would take care of her.

Mandie tried to faint away in order not to face the truth, but busy hands turned her, undressed and bathed her, then re-dressed her as she kept her eyes tightly closed.

Finally another man spoke, "Drink this, Miss Amanda. All of it." Mandie recognized Dr. Woodard as he raised her up from the pillow to swallow the contents of a glass. She obeyed him, and when the glass was empty he laid her back among the pillows and she drifted off to sleep.

Sometime later Mandie, half asleep and with her eyes closed, heard people talking near her.

"This has been too much of a shock—coming home and finding her mother so ill and then hearing about her little brother's death," Dr. Woodard said. "She should have been told when everyone else was."

"I agree with you, Dr. Woodard. There are lots of things she should have been told," a woman said. "I just can't imagine why her grandmother didn't warn her before they got home about the situation here."

"I plan on having a little talk with her grandmother first chance I get," said Dr. Woodard. "Now are you sure you don't mind staying with her? I can send Liza up here, you know."

"No, no, don't do that. Liza already has so much to do. I'll be glad to stay," the woman said. "If I need you I'll let you know."

"I'm pretty sure she'll sleep a while, but when she wakes up she may be hard to handle," Dr. Woodard said. "Don't hesitate to call me if it's necessary."

"I promise I will call you," the woman said.

After a while she whispered, "So you are Amanda."

Mandie drifted off into deep sleep and, when she awoke, saw Liza sitting by her bed. She tried to sit up but found her head was groggy. Why did she feel so terrible? And then she remembered. Polly had told her about Samuel and then had taken her to the cemetery to prove she was right. *Oh, just wait until I confront Grandmother about being kept in the dark about everything!* She planned on doing that immediately and threw back the thin cotton sheet covering her.

"Missy 'Manda, I sees you'se 'wake now," Liza said. Getting up, she bent over the bed and said, "Heah, lemme plump up dese heah pillows fo' you."

Mandie fanned her away with her arms. "No, Liza, I'm going to get up," she told the girl, "if you'll just help me sit up on the side of the bed for a minute until the room quits swinging around."

Liza sighed and put an arm around Mandie. "Go slow now, Missy 'Manda," Liza cautioned her. "Not too fast-like."

Mandie managed to sit straight up on the side of the bed. She closed her eyes for a second and found the room was standing still when she opened them.

"Thanks, Liza," Mandie said. "I don't know why I'm so thick-headed this morning." Liza helped her into her robe, which had been lying on the foot of the bed.

"It be dat sleepin' potion the doctuh man give you last night. De 'fects will wear off when I git yo' some breakfus', which I'll do right now," Liza said, stepping back to look at Mandie.

"Liza, let me see if I can get into a chair before you go out," Mandie said as she slid down from the high bed. She shook her head and steadied herself. "I'll be all right in a minute." She walked to the nearest chair and sat down with a sigh.

"Be sure you stay right there, Missy 'Manda, and I'll go git de food," Liza told her as she left the room. She pushed the door wide open.

Mandie closed her eyes as she leaned back in the big chair. Her little brother was gone forever. If only Dr. Plumbley had known about him he might have been able to save him. The events of last night floated through her mind. Then she remembered hearing Dr. Woodard talking to a woman whose voice she hadn't recognized, but it sounded like the same one who had said, "So you are Amanda," when she first arrived home and went to her room. Who was this woman? Mandie had never even seen her and didn't know what she looked like. *Oh, well,* she thought, *I suppose I'll eventually see her, because she seems to be staying in this house.*

Right now her mind was on her grandmother. Why had she kept everything secret? And when she got home no one told her a thing, not even Joe. He had acted strangely enough that she decided he had been instructed not to tell her anything.

Various thoughts flitted through Mandie's head, but

she kept coming back to the fact that she had lost her little brother. And she felt guilty.

"God, why did you take my little brother away?" she cried to herself. "Why?" She pulled her robe tightly around her and laid her head on the chair pillow. She shook with grief.

Someone touched her shoulder saying, "Mandie."

She turned her head enough to see Joe standing by the chair.

"Mandie, my father told me what happened yesterday, and he said it was all right if I came to talk to you about it," Joe said with a worried look on his face.

Mandie turned her face back into the pillow. "I can't talk, Joe! I just can't!" she cried. "It was all my fault. God took Samuel because of the way I acted. I didn't want him when he was born. All he did was cry and cry and cry all the time."

Joe sat on the arm of the chair and reached to hold Mandie's hand. "Mandie, that's not true. You know that. My father said—"

Mandie turned around to face him and argued, "Yes, it was my fault. It was."

"Listen to me, Mandie," Joe said in a loud, commanding voice as he squeezed her hand hard. "My father said—"

"Your father said there was nothing wrong with him to make him cry like that, that he was just spoiled. And that made me jealous. He had my mother's love and attention all day and all night, and I was left out," Mandie told him in a shaky voice.

"No, Mandie, he wasn't just spoiled. My father later found something terribly wrong with Samuel," Joe told her. "He was in constant pain and would never have grown into a normal child. It was something to do with his back, and nothing could be done for him."

Mandie's eyes and ears were focused on what Joe was saying now. "Something was wrong with Samuel," she repeated. "Something that hurt so much he cried all the time?"

"That's what my father said. He called in a specialist from the state capital to look at him," Joe said. "And the other doctor agreed with my father's opinion."

Mandie thought for a second and then she said, "I don't believe you, Joe Woodard."

"Then talk to my father about it," Joe said. "He'll be able to tell you all the details. It was not your fault that Samuel died."

"It was. It was," Mandie argued.

Liza came in with a tray of hot food and set it on the table next to Mandie. "I wants you to eat ev'ry bite of dis heah food now," she said as she lifted the linen cover. She turned to Joe and said, "And doctuh son, you git back downstairs so's Missy 'Manda kin eat and dress."

"I'll see you again later, Mandie," Joe said as he turned to leave the room.

"Wait, Joe," Mandie called to him. "Do you know where my grandmother is?"

Joe frowned and said, "I believe I heard someone say she had taken a room up on the third floor because she has never had the fever."

"I'll find her then, thanks," Mandie said.

Joe left the room and Mandie picked up the cup of hot coffee Liza had poured from the silver pot.

Liza, perching on another chair nearby, said, "I stays right heah till all dat food be gone. Den I'll he'p you dress, Missy 'Manda."

"Then you might stay here a long time, Liza, because I don't want all that food," Mandie protested, glancing over the hot grits, eggs, bacon, and rolls on the tray. "I only want the coffee and a roll."

"Suit yo'self, Missy 'Manda, but I stay till you done, whatevah you wants to eat," Liza said. "When you gits hungry 'nuff you'll eat a meal."

The strong hot coffee helped clear Mandie's head and warmed her body. She had been icy cold with grief. The hot buttered roll satisfied the gnawing hunger pains in her stomach.

"Liza, I want to get dressed now and go talk to my grandmother," Mandie said, pushing away the tray and standing up. "And I'm not an invalid. You don't have to help me dress."

When she saw Liza's worried face, Mandie realized she had been harsh.

"I'm sorry, Liza, I didn't mean that," Mandie said. "I really do appreciate all that you do for me all the time. But it makes me feel bad when you do so much."

"I don't be doin' 'nuff. Now what dress you be wantin' to put on?" Liza said as she quickly went to open the door to the big chifferobe.

Mandie came up behind her and picked a pink gingham. "This one will do, Liza. I'm not going anywhere, just to see my grandmother," Mandie said as Liza pulled the dress down.

"When you goes to see yo' grandmother, you 'member Grandmother sick wid grief, jes' like you is, Missy 'Manda," Liza reminded her as Mandie shed her nightclothes and pulled on the pink dress.

"But she is to blame for part of mine, Liza, and I am going to ask her why she kept everything a secret from me," Mandie said, quickly brushing her hair.

"Jes' you don't say things you cain't unsay later. 'Member dat. Uncle Ned, he always tell you to think first," Liza reminded her.

"Where is Uncle Ned?" Mandie asked as she plaited her long blonde hair. She remembered Uncle Ned had carried her from the cemetery last night.

"He be 'round downstairs, he and his missus, wid all dem other people," Liza said.

"I'll see him later. Right now I'm going to find my grandmother," Mandie said as she turned to leave the room.

Liza called from where she was picking up the tray, " 'Member what I done tol' you."

Mandie would remember the advice Liza had given her, but remember was all she would do. She planned to have a long talk with her grandmother as soon as she could find her.

In the meantime she hoped Dr. Plumbley had received her message and that he would soon arrive to help her mother.

Chapter 6 / Intruder in the Tunnel

Mandie went through the doorway to the stairs that went up to the third floor and looked up. The window on the landing was pushed up and the shutters were open. The thin curtain moved slightly in the breeze. Evidently someone had decided to clean up and air out the third story, which was seldom used. At the top of the steps she found the door held back by a door prop. The last time she had been up to this floor it had all been closed up and dark.

She had no idea which room her grandmother would be in, so she began peeking in rooms as she went down the corridor. They all seemed to be in use by someone because she saw personal effects in each one. Then she realized all those people downstairs would have to have a place to sleep. They couldn't just sit there all day and all night, too.

At the far end of the hallway she silently opened the door to the corner bedroom, which she knew was larger than the others and which also had its own sitting room. This was the right room, but her grandmother was asleep on the sofa. She was fully dressed, and Mandie could tell by the food tray on the table nearby that she evidently had already been up and had breakfast in her room.

Not daring to wake her, Mandie turned to tiptoe out of the room. Snowball came racing into the room just then and she almost tripped over him. He let out a loud meow and Mandie snatched him up and hurried out into the hallway, closing the door behind her.

"Snowball, you are always causing me trouble," Mandie whispered as she cuddled the white cat in her arms. "If Grandmother had woke up she would have been awfully angry with us. You shouldn't be on this floor anyhow."

Mandie carried Snowball down to the second floor and closed the door to the stairs behind her. She put him down and said, "Now you can roam around all you want on this floor, but don't you go back up there, you hear?"

Snowball seemed to be listening to every word as he sat there and looked at her. Then he jumped up and scampered down the corridor.

Mandie went back to her room. She didn't want to face all those people downstairs.

Liza was dusting and straightening up when Mandie opened the door. The Negro girl stopped to look at Mandie when she entered the room and asked, "Well?"

Mandie sighed as she flopped in a chair. "Well, my grandmother was asleep on the sofa in her sitting room," she said. "Liza, do those people downstairs have rooms on the third floor, too?"

"Dat's right, and dey ain't got no maid service neithuh, 'cause Mistuh John, he tell dem dey have to do fo' theirselves, being Aunt Lou is tied up wid yo' mother and

I be tied up wid you," Liza said as she continued dusting. "And I has to he'p Jenny wid de cookin', what de neighbors don't bring in."

"Liza, you have so much to do, you don't have to do things for me. I didn't realize how busy everybody is," Mandie said. "Maybe I could do something to help." She got up and reached for the duster in Liza's hand. "Something like clean up my own room."

Liza moved away from her reach. "No, no, Missy 'Manda, you be my number one job," Liza protested. "And I intend doin' my job." She looked around the room. "Now bein' ev'rything is in order heah, I go he'p Jenny till you needs me."

As Liza opened the door, Mandie decided it would be too lonely here in her room with no one to talk to, so she asked, "Liza, if you see Uncle Ned around and he's not busy, ask him if he would come up and talk to me, please."

"Dat I'll do, Missy 'Manda," Liza promised, closing the door behind her.

Mandie got up, opened the door, and wandered out into the hallway where there was a window seat. There was no one about, so she sat down to stare out the window and think.

It was all she could do to restrain herself from going to her mother's room. But she realized she might get the fever herself and cause more work and anxiety. If only Dr. Plumbley would hurry up and come from New York!

Then she thought about what Joe had told her regarding Samuel's health. She didn't believe it at all. It was just his way of keeping her from blaming herself. And she was to blame. She had not wanted Samuel. He had come between her and her mother. And now she was sure God was punishing her for the bad things she had done.

"Oh, Samuel, I did love you. I truly did," she said to herself as her blue eyes filled with tears.

She didn't hear Uncle Ned's soft step on the carpet until he sat down beside her on the window seat.

"Papoose feel better?" the old man asked as he looked at her closely.

Mandie hastily pulled a handkerchief from her pocket and wiped her eyes. "I suppose so, Uncle Ned," she said. "But it's hard to feel better with all the terrible things happening to us." Then she broke into tears again and put her head on Uncle Ned's shoulder. "Uncle Ned, nobody told me anything. It was all a shock. Why didn't you let me know what was going on?"

The old Indian put an arm around Mandie and hugged her tight. "Sorry, Papoose. Grandmother say we not tell you. Make you worry and sick on journey home," he explained. "I tell her, Senator tell her: must tell Papoose. But she say no."

Mandie straightened up to look at him as she said, "My grandmother didn't want me to worry on the way home, but everybody else knew. How did she think I would feel walking into all this sadness and worry? At least I could have prepared myself for it."

"I know, Papoose. I know. I tell her that, but she say no and she is boss," Uncle Ned said sadly.

Mandie had a sudden spiteful idea. "Uncle Ned, I have a secret that I've decided I'm not going to share with Grandmother because she didn't share anything with me," Mandie told him as she wiped her eyes again.

"Papoose must not do spiteful things," Uncle Ned said.

"It's not a spiteful thing, Uncle Ned. It's something I've done that my grandmother doesn't know about and which might not even work out, but I'm hoping with all my heart that it will," Mandie replied as she glanced out the window.

"Papoose must think about this thing she's done," he said.

Mandie looked up at his old wrinkled face and made a quick decision. "I'll tell you what I've done, Uncle Ned," she began. "Remember Dr. Plumbley, the Negro man who is our friend? He lives in New York? Well, I went to the telegraph office yesterday and sent him a wire, asking him to come and doctor my mother since Dr. Woodard said he had done all he could do." She watched for his reaction.

Uncle Ned was surprised and he said, "Papoose, this doctor man has sick people in New York. He cannot leave them to come all the way down here."

"I know he has patients up there," Mandie said. "But he'll make arrangements with another doctor so he can come. You wait and see. He will come." She reached for Uncle Ned's wrinkled hand. "Uncle Ned, he's got to come. That's the only hope for my mother."

"No, no, Papoose, not *only* hope. Remember, Big God in charge," Uncle Ned said.

"I know, Uncle Ned, but I'm hoping God will give Dr. Plumbley the knowledge to cure my mother," Mandie said. She was silent for a moment as she thought about how this had come about, and she decided to share this with her friend. She shifted her position to turn and face the old man. "Uncle Ned, do you believe in angels?"

Uncle Ned smiled at her and replied, "Big God has lots of angels."

"But have you ever seen one?" she asked.

"Angels not seeable, Papoose," he said.

"Oh, but I saw one! It was in my room the first night when I came home, and it spoke to me," Mandie said, looking at him.

"Spoke to Papoose?" he questioned her.

"Yes, and it said, 'Peace. You will know. You will know.' Just like that," Mandie said. "I finally figured out what I would *know*. Something just told me to go wire Dr. Plumbley and I did and then I felt better. That's what the angel meant for me to do."

"Papoose, maybe dream this," he said.

"No, I thought about that, too, but it was too real. I believe I really saw an angel," Mandie said. "And the angel came to help me help my mother."

"What angel look like?" he asked.

"There was a real bright light around it and I couldn't see its features, so I don't know for sure whether it was a man or a woman, but it seemed to be young. I was ... petrified. I couldn't speak until it spoke to me. It was as if it had a secret and I was holding my breath to hear what it was. As soon as it spoke I felt warm and hopeful. It was a strange feeling," Mandie said, squinting her eyes as she remembered.

When Uncle Ned didn't speak for a few moments, Mandie felt that for one time the old man had nothing to say. Evidently he didn't know whether to agree with her or not.

Mandie had another thought. "Uncle Ned, do you know how long it takes the train to get here from New York?" she asked.

The old man shook his head. "Do not know, Papoose. New York long way," he said.

Liza interrupted them as she came rushing down the hallway, waving an envelope in her hand. "Missy 'Manda, you'se got a message all de way from Noo Yawk. See heah!" she was yelling as she came up to them and handed Mandie the envelope. She stood waiting to see what this was all about.

Mandie excitedly opened the envelope and pulled out a small sheet of paper, from which she read aloud, "Will come first train possible. Samuel Hezekiah Plumbley." She hugged Uncle Ned and added, "I knew he would! I knew he would!" Tears of joy ran down her cheeks.

Uncle Ned patted her blonde head. "Papoose must pray Big God give this doctor man knowledge to make mother of Papoose well again," he said.

"Yes, we must," Mandie said, straightening up and reaching for Uncle Ned's hand. Suddenly she saw Liza still standing there and she grabbed her hand. "Liza, we have to pray for this doctor from New York. You remember him coming to visit us, don't you?"

Liza nodded. "I sho' does," she said. "And he comin' heah agin?"

"Yes, he's coming to doctor my mother," Mandie said, and then added, "But, Liza, this is our secret. I don't want you to tell anyone, understand?"

"I understands, Missy 'Manda, jes' you and me and Injun man knows 'bout dis," she said.

"You pray, Uncle Ned," Mandie told him.

Looking upward, the old Indian began, "Big God, please give this doctor man knowledge to make mother of Papoose well."

Mandie repeated the prayer after him and Liza joined in.

Then Mandie jumped up and walked back and forth across the hallway. "I'm so happy that he's coming," she said.

"What dis Doctuh Woodard gwine do when dis other doctuh git heah? He gwine leave?" Liza asked. "And he gwine take doctuh son Joe wid him?"

Mandie stopped and gasped. "I hadn't thought about that," she said.

"Papoose must tell him New York doctor man coming," Uncle Ned said.

Mandie suddenly wondered what Dr. Woodard would say when he found out what she had done. He might be awfully angry with her. "Not right now," she said. "I'll tell Dr. Woodard later."

"Do not forget, Papoose," Uncle Ned said sternly. "Must tell."

"I'll remember, Uncle Ned," Mandie said. Turning to Liza, she asked, "Does anyone else know I got a message from New York?"

"Not a soul, Missy 'Manda. I answers door, man gives me dis heah enbellope and say, 'Message from Noo Yawk for Miss 'Manda Shaw.' I takes it and runs all de way up heah," Liza explained.

"That's good, Liza. Just remember to keep it a secret," Mandie reminded her.

"Dat I do. Now I got to go back and he'p Jenny in de kitchen," Liza replied, then hurried down the hallway.

Uncle Ned stood up. "I go, too," he said. "Chop wood for cookstove."

"And I'm going back upstairs to see if my grandmother is awake," Mandie said as she also stood up.

Uncle Ned paused to look at her as he said, "Papoose must remember to *think*." He went on down the hallway.

Mandie walked back into her room and went to stand by the window. So many things were piling up for her to think about. Uncle Ned had told her to think. And now she thought about Dr. Woodard. What would she tell him? And if he got angry with her, wouldn't Joe also be angry? After all, Dr. Woodard was Joe's father. She'd just have to wait a while before she told him that Dr. Plumbley was coming because she'd have to plan what she would say.

Then there was her problem with her grandmother.

She was going to ask her why she had kept everything secret. And she might as well go on and do that now.

She climbed the stairs to the third floor again and went directly to the rooms her grandmother was occupying. She peeked inside and saw that her grandmother was still asleep on the sofa.

Mandie silently closed the door as she said to herself, "Oh, well, I'll come back again."

She wandered down the long corridor and happened to pass Uncle John's library. The door was partly open. She knew the door was kept locked and no one was allowed inside because this was where her uncle kept all his business papers.

Frowning, Mandie paused to look through the crack, thinking maybe Uncle John was inside. But instead she saw a black-haired woman pulling back the draperies in the corner of the room. As Mandie watched, the woman took a key from her pocket, inserted it in the door behind the draperies and unlocked it. Then she pushed the latch on the paneled wall inside the opening and the wall slid away, revealing the steps to the secret tunnel. Mandie gasped, wondering who the woman was.

Without even thinking, Mandie rushed into the library to stop the woman. But before she could reach her, Mandie saw the door close and heard the key click in the lock.

"Who are you? What are you doing in there?" Mandie demanded as she knocked on the door.

Only silence met her ears. "I'll catch her at the other end," Mandie said aloud to herself.

She quickly ran down the stairs all the way to the first floor and out the back entrance. She continued down the hill behind the house to the woods below. Once there, she found the entrance to the end of the tunnel. She slipped behind a large bush to a place where she could see the door and wait for the woman to come out.

Mandie waited and waited and nothing happened until Snowball came prowling through the bushes. She picked him up and brushed leaves from his fur.

"It's good to be home where you can run free and I don't have to worry about putting a leash on you," she murmured to the cat as she held him close.

Finally Mandie decided the woman wasn't coming out of the tunnel and she stepped out of the bushes to go back up to the house. She almost collided with Joe.

"Well, what are you doing here?" Mandie asked as she set Snowball down.

"I get tired sitting around the house with nobody to talk to, so I thought I'd go for a walk," he said as he looked away into the distance.

"I know. I've been in my room just about ever since I got home," Mandie agreed. Then she remembered why she was at this particular place. "I saw a woman in Uncle John's library unlock the door to the tunnel, go inside, and lock it behind her. I figured I'd catch her when she came out down here and find out who she is and how she got that key, and also how she knew about the secret tunnel."

"You didn't know who she was?" Joe asked.

"I've never seen her before that I know of, but then, according to Liza, the house is full kinpeople that I've never seen," Mandie replied.

"Then maybe she's a relative," Joe suggested.

"Well, even if she is a relative, how did she get into Uncle John's library? You know how strict he is about keeping it locked and not allowing anyone else in there," Mandie said. Her arm itched, and as she rubbed it, she noticed that a bush had scratched it.

"Maybe she's someone your Uncle John knows pretty

well, and he let her into the library," Joe said. He reached to touch Mandie's arm as he said, "It's scratched, but luckily it didn't cut enough to bleed." Before Mandie knew it, Joe had grasped her hand in his.

Mandie couldn't decide what to do. She wasn't used to Joe doing such things. But then he seemed concerned about her after all the sadness she'd been experiencing. She didn't pull free but her voice wavered as she said, "I'll wash the scratch when I go back to my room."

Joe looked into her blue eyes and said in a solemn voice, "Mandie, I want you to know I feel for you. You've borne all this better than I ever could have."

Mandie did pull her hand free as she looked around and said, "Let's talk about something else. Like where did that woman go? Maybe we could catch her coming back out of Uncle John's library if we hurry. She has to come out somewhere."

Joe, smiling at being included in the adventure, said, "Let's go!"

They hurried up to the third floor and down the hall-way to Uncle John's library. The door was closed, and when Mandie tried it she found it was locked.

"Oh, shucks! I should have come back sooner," Mandie said with a sigh.

"How could you, when you were thinking she would come out the other entrance to the tunnel?" Joe said. "Anyhow, if you see her again, let me know and I'll find out who she is."

"I'm not sure I'd recognize her. I didn't see her face, only her back, and she had black hair," Mandie explained as they stood there in the hallway.

"There must be at least ten women in the house who have black hair," Joe said. "What was she wearing?"

"Black. I believe everything she wore was black," Mandie said.

"Then she must be a relative, because all your kin-people are in mourning for your little brother," Joe said, looking at Mandie.

Mandie frowned, closed her eyes, and then turned to walk down the hallway. "Maybe I'll get a better look if she comes back to Uncle John's library," she said as they went down the stairs to the second floor.

All the time Mandie was thinking, *Maybe I could just tell Joe that Dr. Plumbley is coming and he could tell his father. But what will I say? How will I do this?*

When they came to the door to Mandie's room, Joe asked, "Would you want to sit out here on the window seat and talk for a while?"

"I'm trying to catch my grandmother to discuss some things with her, but every time I go up to her room she is asleep on the sofa in her sitting room. I suppose I'll just go back up and try again," Mandie said.

"Then maybe you'll come downstairs later," Joe said.

"No, I don't want to see all those strangers," Mandie protested. "I just don't feel like facing them right now."

"Would it be all right if I come back up later then?" Joe asked.

Mandie looked up at him. Joe was two years older than Mandie and was tall and thin, with a determined chin. "I'll let you know. Liza comes up here every so often and I'll tell her to give you a message if I can have you come, because I don't know when I'll be able to catch Grandmother," she said.

"All right. I'll be downstairs," Joe said as he went on down the hallway.

As soon as he turned the corner, Mandie went back up to the third floor and down the hall to her grandmother's rooms. This time the door was ajar.

Aha! She's up now, Mandie thought to herself. *I'll catch her this time.*

She hurried to the door and pushed it open. She looked around the sitting room. Her grandmother was not on the sofa. Evidently she was in her bedroom. Mandie went on inside to the door of the bedroom. When she looked in, she was disappointed because Mrs. Taft was nowhere to be found.

Mandie left the rooms and started back down the stairs. "She's probably downstairs with all those people, but I'll catch up with her soon," she said to herself.

But Mrs. Taft was not downstairs with all those people. When Mandie pushed open the door to her own room, she found her grandmother sitting in a chair by the window.

Chapter 7 / Mandie and Joe Explore

Mandie was so surprised at seeing her grandmother sitting in her room, she couldn't think of a thing to say. She sat down in a chair opposite Mrs. Taft.

They silently looked at each other and finally Mrs. Taft spoke. "I have been terribly wrong, dear, in not keeping you informed of the situation here at home," she said in a trembly voice. "I came to ask you for forgiveness. Dr. Woodard told me everything last night."

Tears blurred Mandie's eyes, and forgetting all her anger, she rushed into her grandmother's arms. Mandie sat beside her on the arm of the chair and they both cried.

"Grandmother, I need your forgiveness, too. I've been awfully angry with you and was planning how to get even. I'm sorry," Mandie said as she straightened up to look into her grandmother's face.

"Then, we're both forgiven," Mrs. Taft said, dabbing her eyes with a lacy handkerchief. "Oh, Amanda, what a sad time. We've not only lost your little brother, but Dr. Woodard has done all he can for your mother. What are we going to do if—if we lose her, too. I just can't take any more."

Mandie's own grief was arrested as she realized her grandmother needed her help and encouragement. She would have to be the one to offer comfort. Her grandmother was in terrible shape. She quickly decided to tell her about Dr. Plumbley.

"Grandmother, Dr. Woodard may have done all he can, but I wired Dr. Plumbley," Mandie began, trying to act more optimistic than she felt. "Remember, he's the old friend of the Shaw family who went to New York to study and practice medicine? Well, he wired me back that he is coming—"

Mrs. Taft took her handkerchief away from her eyes to look at Mandie. "I remember the name, dear, but do you think he would know more than Dr. Woodard does about the fever?"

"Oh, yes, Grandmother," Mandie said. She was thinking about the angel's visit and the message it had given her that caused her to wire the doctor. She quickly decided now was not the time to share this with her grandmother. "After all," she continued, "he's been studying at the most modern schools of medicine in New York, and although I love Dr. Woodard dearly, I don't think he's as up-to-date as Dr. Plumbley must be."

"We'll see, dear, but he'll have to act as an advisor to Dr. Woodard. We can't dismiss Dr. Woodard after all his many, many years of caring for the family," Mrs. Taft said, and then she tried to smile. "Maybe Dr. Plumbley will be the answer to my prayers." She squeezed Mandie's hand.

"Mine, too, Grandmother, and Uncle Ned's, too. I told him about Dr. Plumbley," Mandie said. "And Liza knows because she was the one who received the wire from him and brought it up to me."

"I suppose we'll have to let Dr. Woodard know, too," Mrs. Taft said, drying her eyes. "Or have you mentioned it to him?"

Mandie got up to walk around the room. "No, I haven't yet, Grandmother, but I promise I will. I just haven't gotten up the nerve yet," she said, pausing to look out the window as she considered her problem.

"Well, we have plenty of time, dear. It takes quite a while to get here from New York and then, too, Dr. Woodard stays busy," Mrs. Taft said, straightening her clothes.

There was a light tap on the door and Mandie called, "Come in."

Liza entered the room as she announced, "It be eatin' time in dis heah house." She stopped when she saw Mrs. Taft. "Would y'all be wantin' me to bring both yo' trays in heah and y'all eat together now?"

Mandie and Mrs. Taft looked at each other.

"I really should go downstairs and speak to the kinpeople, but I just haven't been able to yet," Mrs. Taft began.

"Neither have I," Mandie said quickly. "So why don't we eat here?"

"That would be fine, dear," Mrs. Taft said. "I really don't want much of anything, but I suppose we'll have to eat something in order to survive."

Liza turned to leave and then added, "Missy 'Manda, dat doctuh son be worryin' me to death wantin' to know if you had sent him a message."

"He wanted to come up here and sit on the window seat out there in the hallway with me, and I told him I'd get you to give him the message later," Mandie explained.

"Amanda, why don't we ask him to eat here with us?

I imagine he's at loose ends down there," Mrs. Taft suggested.

"Of course, Grandmother," Mandie agreed, wondering what they would talk about with her grandmother present. "Liza, please tell him to come, but he can bring his own tray since you won't let me help you."

"I'm right sho' he'll be glad to do dat," Liza told them as she left the room.

"I don't know why Joe came here in the middle of all this sickness," Mandie said, sitting near her grandmother. "I'm so afraid somebody else will get it."

"According to Dr. Woodard, Joe had the fever when he was small," Mrs. Taft said.

"Grandmother, is it true that if you've had the fever before, you won't get it again?" Mandie asked.

"That's the common belief, dear," Mrs. Taft said. "But, you know, we've never had the fever much in this area over the years, and people around here don't really know much about it."

"I don't think I've ever had it," Mandie said. "Dr. Woodard might know since he's always been our doctor."

"No, you haven't had the fever," Mrs. Taft told her. "As soon as Dr. Woodard saw us come home he told me to keep you away from your mother." Her voice trembled. "I suppose I haven't looked after you at all."

"Grandmother, I'm thirteen years old, you know, and that makes me old enough to look after myself," Mandie reminded her. She wanted to ask her how Samuel had caught the fever, but it was too heartbreaking to talk about that. Evidently her mother had caught the fever from Samuel.

"I know you are growing up, dear, but I do hate to think about the time when you'll be out on your own, married, and perhaps with little ones for you to look after,"

Mrs. Taft said. "So I'll just take care of you as long as you need me."

Mandie smiled slightly at her grandmother and said, "I do still need you to look after me at school when it comes to dealing with Miss Prudence."

Mrs. Taft didn't smile back, but her eyes twinkled as she said, "Now, that's a different story. Miss Prudence means well, I'm sure, but she is absolutely unbendable."

Liza arrived with a large tray. "I put dis right heah and then I gits de other one," she said as she set the tray on the table nearby. "Be right back."

And she was right back with another tray. Mandie looked puzzled and asked, "Liza, where did you get the second tray? You couldn't have gone all the way to the kitchen and back that fast."

Liza put her hands on her hips and looked at Mandie as she said, "Why, Missy 'Manda, you knows I ain't gwine carry dese heah trays up and down de stairs. Dat dumbwaiter do dat fo' me."

"Oh, I had forgotten there was a dumbwaiter down the hallway. We've never used it since I've lived here that I know of," Mandie said with a little laugh.

Joe came in at that moment with a tray and placed it on the table beside the others. Looking at Mandie and then at her grandmother, he said, "Thanks for asking me up to eat. It's not much fun eating with a bunch of strangers."

Liza spoke up and said, "I done tol' you Jenny let you eat in de kitchen wid her if'n you be skeered of dem people."

"No, Jenny won't let me. I tried it and she said, 'You git out of my kitchen and back in dat dining room wheah y'all belong.' So you see, she didn't want me in there," Joe said with a smile. "Guess I'll have to start going next door and eating with Polly. She wouldn't mind."

"Oh, no, you don't!" Liza said emphatically.

Mandie knew Joe was teasing Liza. Polly was known to have a great interest in Joe. She flirted with him every chance she got.

"Be anything else, Miz Taft?" Liza asked as she uncovered the lady's tray.

"No, thank you, Liza, this is more than I'll ever eat," Mrs. Taft said, surveying the contents of the tray.

"We'll put the trays on the dumbwaiter when we're finished, Liza, so you won't have to come all the way back up here," Mandie told her.

"Jes' pull dat bell over theah if you be needin' me," Liza said as she left the room. Mandie knew she was referring to a rope-pull over on the other side of her room that rang a bell in the kitchen.

There was very little conversation as the three nibbled on their food. No one seemed to have an appetite.

"Would you like to go outside for some fresh air after we finish eating?" Joe asked Mandie.

Before she could answer, Mrs. Taft spoke up. "Yes, Amanda, you do need to get out of the house for a little while," she said as she drank her coffee.

"Do you want to come with us, Grandmother? We could go down the back steps without getting tangled up with all those people downstairs," Mandie suggested.

"No, dear, I'll just go back to my room and rest. Maybe later I'll venture outside," Mrs. Taft said. "I'll stay around where I can be in touch with Dr. Woodard."

Joe finished off the potatoes on his plate and Mandie ate a roll as she watched him. She wanted to tell him that Dr. Plumbley was coming but she didn't know how to break the news. She didn't know when Dr. Plumbley would arrive but she felt time was running out.

"Joe, does your father have other patients who have the fever now?" she asked.

"No, as far as I know, nobody in this district has had it except your family," Joe said. "That's why my father can spend so much time with your mother. No other case is as urgent as the fever."

"We appreciate the time and effort your father has spent here, Joe," Mrs. Taft said.

Mandie quickly looked at her. She thought her grandmother might be going to tell Joe about Dr. Plumbley, but she didn't. And Mandie decided the best thing she could do was get Joe away from her grandmother before something was said about the other doctor coming from New York. Her grandmother had already laid down her napkin and Mandie quickly folded hers and put it on her tray.

"Well, I suppose I'm ready to go outside," Mandie said as her grandmother stood up.

"Y'all go ahead, dear. I'll see you later in the day," Mrs. Taft told them as she walked toward the door. "Don't forget to take the trays, Amanda."

"Yes, ma'am," Mandie said as Mrs. Taft went on into the corridor. She picked up her tray and Joe brought his.

They hurried to the dumbwaiter with them. It was like a tiny elevator that was pulled up and down by ropes from the kitchen.

"You stay here and hold the rope and I'll get the other tray," Joe told her.

Mandie waited, and when he came back she made a suggestion. "Let's get the key to the tunnel from Mr. Jason and walk through it to get outside," she said.

"We'll have to go downstairs to find him," Joe said. "He's probably eating right now."

"Joe, would you please find him and get the key so I

don't have to go down there?" Mandie asked.

"Sure, Mandie, I'll be right back," Joe said. "Wait for me at the window seat outside your room." He hurried down the hallway.

Mandie went to sit on the window seat. She thought about the woman she had seen entering the tunnel earlier. She wondered again who the woman was. Very few people knew about the tunnel. Mandie's great-grandfather had built the passageway to hide the Cherokees who wanted to stay in North Carolina when their tribe was being forced to leave in 1838. The house was constructed at that time and he had added the tunnel.

When Joe returned, Mandie half expected him to say Jason Bond didn't have the key because she knew the woman had a key, but he held it up as he came toward her. He was carrying a lantern, too.

"I'm glad Mr. Jason had the key. I was afraid that woman still had it," Mandie said as she stood up.

"Oh, no, Mr. Bond didn't know anything about that woman. I asked him. He said he has had the key all the time, that nobody had borrowed it," Joe explained.

"That's a puzzle. The only other key that I know of is on Uncle John's key ring, and since he's with my mother, I don't believe anyone would go in there and ask to borrow it." Mandie pondered the problem as they walked up the stairs to the third floor.

Joe pulled another key out of his pocket. "Remember, there are actually two keys that you need to have to get into the tunnel, one to your uncle John's library door, which is this one." He held up the key from his pocket. "And this one here unlocks the door to the tunnel." He held up the other key in his hand.

Mandie stopped to think, then said, "You're right. I've been saying the key to the tunnel all this time, but that woman had to unlock the library with one key and then have the other one to unlock the tunnel. I wonder how she did that."

Joe looked back and said, "Let's go." He waited for her at the top of the staircase.

Mandie caught up, and when she tried the doorknob to Uncle John's library she half expected the door to be unlocked, but it wasn't. Joe set the lantern down, inserted the key, and opened the heavy door.

There were shelves filled with books on three sides of the room. In front of a large stained-glass window stood Uncle John's huge desk. All the shutters were open and Mandie quickly glanced around, thinking that woman might even be in this room, but there was nobody there.

Mandie looked past the carved couch across the room to the draperies in the corner. They were pulled over the door to the tunnel and she quickly tugged at the cords and opened them. There was a smaller door behind them, and Joe set the lantern down again to try a key in the lock. It opened and revealed a paneled wall.

Mandie rushed forward. "Let me. Please," she told Joe. He stood aside as she pushed a latch on the paneled wall and one panel swung aside, showing the entrance to the secret tunnel.

"Hold it open while I light the lantern," Joe told her. He took matches from his pocket and got the light going. "Now."

Mandie, still holding back the panel, stepped aside and allowed Joe to enter with the lantern first. Then she followed and the panel swung closed.

"I had forgotten how dark it is in here," Mandie said, and then she gasped. "If that woman I saw come in here was carrying a light of any kind, I don't remember seeing it."

Joe swung the lantern around and then said, "There's another lantern, right there." He moved close to where it was sitting just inside the doorway.

Mandie thought for a moment and said, "Well, then, if she used that lantern she had to have come back out from this entrance."

Joe grinned at her and said, "Right."

"I should have come back up to the house instead of staying down there in the woods so long watching the other end of the tunnel," Mandie said.

"Are we going on through?" Joe asked, starting down the steps into the tunnel.

"Oh, yes, let's do," Mandie said, catching up.

The tunnel was on several levels through the house and on down into the ground. Mandie and Joe went down lots of steps, through dark rooms, and they were about halfway down when they stopped to talk.

"This place has always been amazing to me, the way it's built," Joe remarked.

"It sure took a lot of hard work," Mandie agreed.

They were standing in a small room that had heavy wooden benches along the walls. They knew the door on the far side led to more steps going downward and through more rooms.

"You ought to think of some purpose for this tunnel now, Mandie," Joe told her as he swung the lantern around.

The light in the lantern suddenly flickered and went out. There was a squeaking sound, like a door was being opened. Mandie grabbed hold of Joe's arm.

"Joe! You got any more matches?" she whispered.

Joe whispered back, "A pocketful, but let's listen first to see what that noise was."

Mandie held her breath as she squeezed Joe's arm.

Joe took her hand in his free one and held it tight. They didn't move.

It was so dark Mandie's eyes couldn't penetrate the darkness. And it was so silent she could hear Joe breathing. After a few moments she whispered, "Let's get going."

Joe lit the lantern and they looked around. There was nobody there. They silently, slowly moved forward and began descending the next set of steps.

When they reached the end of the tunnel they found the outside door standing open. Mandie ran forward to check the nail where the key ordinarily hung. The key was there.

"This gets more complicated all the time," Mandie remarked as she looked about. "Somebody must have unlocked the door, hung the key back up, and then left, leaving the door open."

"Or else they had another key to this door," Joe said, examining the lock.

"If that woman had keys to the library and the entrance upstairs, then she probably has a key to this door, too," Mandie said, going through the open door. Joe extinguished the lantern and followed.

The bushes were thick around the doorway, and when they pushed ahead through them, a piece of black ribbon hanging on a bush caught Mandie's eye. She stooped to pick it off from the branch.

"Look! That woman was wearing black. She probably lost this ribbon," Mandie told Joe as they examined it.

"It does look clean and fresh. Someone must have lost it recently," Joe said.

"I hope we can catch up with her," Mandie remarked.

"One way you could do that is to come downstairs part of the time instead of staying in your room, and look the people over to see whether you find her among them," Joe suggested.

Mandie shook her head and said, "I wouldn't recognize her because I didn't see her face. Of course I might remember the back of her hair or her dress or something."

"So are you coming inside the house now where the visitors are, or are you going up the back stairs to your room?" Joe asked as they started walking toward the house.

"I have to go to my room for a while because no one would know where to find me out here if they needed me," Mandie said, thinking of the coming arrival of Dr. Plumbley. "Maybe later I'll go downstairs."

Joe stopped suddenly and said, "I just thought of something. We should have locked the outside door to the tunnel down there."

"You're right," Mandie agreed. "But what would we do with the key? It's supposed to stay on the nail by the door."

Joe thought for a moment and then said, "I tell you what. You go ahead, since you're going to your room, and I'll go back, lock the door, and take the key to Mr. Bond when I give him these two keys."

"Thanks, Joe," Mandie said. "I'll see you later."

"Right," Joe said as he began walking back to the tunnel exit.

Mandie rushed up the back stairs and into her room without seeing anyone. She began walking the floor, wondering when Dr. Plumbley would arrive and what she would say to Dr. Woodard. This was so important to her that she didn't even stop to think about the noise they had heard in the tunnel and the door being left open.

Chapter 8 / The Train Schedule

Mandie stopped pacing the floor of her bedroom and spoke aloud to herself, "I could at least go to the depot and find out when the train comes in from New York. Now, why didn't I think of that before?"

She quickly tied on the bonnet that matched her dress. The sunshine was hot outside and the bonnet would also help conceal her face. This time she picked up her small drawstring purse, because she remembered going to send the wire and not having any money with her. However, there would probably be no reason for it this time.

When she was ready to leave, she stopped with a sigh and said, "What now?" as someone softly tapped on her door. Hastily removing her bonnet and placing it and her purse on a table nearby, she went to see who it was.

Polly was standing outside her door. "Can I come in for a minute?" the girl asked. "This is the first chance I've had to get back up here. There's always someone around when I try to slip inside your house."

"Oh, all right, Polly, come on in," Mandie said with another sigh as she pushed the door open. "But remember, if you come down with the fever it won't be my fault."

Polly shrugged and came into the room and sat in a chair. Mandie closed the door and looked at her. "Did you want anything special?" Mandie asked. "I mean, is there a special reason for your visit?"

Polly looked at her with a frown as she said, "Of course, Mandie. I wanted to know if you were all right after that visit we made to the cemetery."

Mandie sat on the bed. "Yes, I'm all right, Polly, but all that was a terrible shock," she said sadly. "I just can't . . . believe . . . that little Samuel . . . is gone." Her voice trembled.

"I'm sorry, Mandie," Polly told her. "I hope your mother is better."

"Her condition hasn't changed," Mandie said. "She's no better, but she's no worse. I'm just hoping and praying that she'll make it." She dropped her eyes so Polly couldn't see the tears.

"Is there anything I can do, Mandie? Anything at all?" Polly asked in a quiet voice.

Mandie suddenly had an idea, and she replied, "Polly, someone has been in the tunnel and they left the door open down at the end in the woods. I haven't been able to catch them. Joe and I found it open this afternoon. If you could kinda help watch, you'd be doing me a favor."

Polly's face brightened as she asked, "Are you and Joe going back down there?"

"No, I'm not, but I have an idea Joe will be hanging around, hoping to see someone," Mandie replied. "He didn't actually say he would, but I felt he would do some investigating on his own after I came back to my room here." Mandie knew Polly was smitten with Joe and she was using this scheme to get Polly out of her room so she could check the train schedule.

Polly stood up and asked, "Should I go down there right now?"

Mandie shrugged her shoulders nonchalantly as she replied, "If you want to."

As Polly hastily went to the door, she stopped to ask, "And if I see anyone going in or coming out of the tunnel what am I supposed to do?"

"Look them over real good so you'll recognize them when you see them again, then come and let me know," Mandie said as she followed Polly into the hallway.

"Hadn't I better watch to see where they go if they're coming out? If they're going in, you know I'll never follow them into that dark place," Polly explained.

"All right," Mandie said. "But you'd better get Joe to go with you if you start following somebody around. Now, why don't you go see where Joe is so he can help you watch?"

"Of course, Mandie. See you later," Polly said as she hurried down the hallway.

Mandie went back into her room and waited long enough for Polly to get out of the house. Then she put her bonnet back on and picked up her purse. She didn't want to run into Joe and she was hoping Polly would find him. Of course, knowing Polly, if Joe was to be found she would find him.

Mandie didn't see anyone as she quietly left the house by the back entrance into the garden. Walking briskly she went around the block to keep from going in front of the house. As she turned the last corner toward the depot, she stopped in surprise and then ducked into the entrance of a store. There was Abraham, her uncle John's yard man, rattling along in his wagon, headed in the direction of the depot.

"I hope he goes on past the train station," she said aloud to herself. "I can't imagine what he would be doing going to the depot anyhow." She watched from behind the corner of the store front as Abraham drove on down the street. And she breathed a sigh of relief as he went on past the depot, turned the corner, and disappeared.

"I'll have to hurry. He might come back," Mandie said to herself. She rushed on down the street to the depot and went inside the small waiting room. There was no one there, and there was no clerk behind the window. She looked around, not sure what to do now.

Finally walking up to the glass window at the counter, she called, "Anyone here? Is there anyone here?" There was only silence. She couldn't see into the small room behind the window.

She bit her lip and, with a sigh, walked out onto the platform to look around. There was nobody anywhere.

"Well, did everyone just quit and go home?" she said loudly as she stomped her foot.

"Yessum," a man's voice said, and she whirled around to see an old man in workclothes in the trainyard on the other side of the platform. "That clerk, he's gone home fer a bite to eat, seein' ain't no train comin' in till late today," the man went on as he loaded freight onto a cart sitting on a side track.

Mandie quickly walked to the other side of the platform and called to him, "What time does the train from New York get in here?"

"Depends on what changes you make up the road," the man said, straightening up to look at Mandie. "They's diff'runt trains come in from up north."

Mandie was puzzled as she asked, "How are you supposed to know when to meet someone coming in from New York then?"

"I s'pect you jest keep meetin' all the trains from the north, miss," he said. "And all them trains done come in today. We're waitin' fer the trains from the south this afternoon."

"So, in other words, a person coming from New York would come in on a train from the north and all the trains from the north come in before this time of day," Mandie said.

"Not always, 'cause sometimes they're late, hours late," the man said as he continued loading the cart.

"Thank you," Mandie called as she turned to walk down the platform. She went back through the empty waiting room and out into the street.

She stopped to look around outside as she mumbled to herself, "And I thought trains had to run on a fixed schedule, otherwise they'd run into each other. And the clerk just leaves the place empty and goes home for dinner. What a mess!"

Mandie kept alert for any sign of Abraham as she hurried up the street. She was able to get all the way back home and almost to the back entrance without seeing anyone she knew. Then as she slipped through the tall stalks of corn in the garden, she heard a woman's voice speaking, "So you are Amanda."

Anxious to get up to her room, Mandie broke into a run to the back door. She glanced around but never did see anyone. She didn't stop until she was in her room. Then she tossed off her bonnet and flopped onto a chair to get her breath.

She was beginning to feel strange about the woman's voice she had heard several times. So far she had not even had a glimpse of her. And why did the woman keep saying the same thing, "So you are Amanda"? Was she imagining she heard a woman speaking? Or was the woman real? She had too many things on her mind to ponder this question long.

Her thoughts returned to the train schedule. There didn't seem to be any definite time that she could look for a train from New York. Dr. Plumbley would probably just come walking up to the door without anyone expecting him.

And as she thought of him she wondered how her mother was. Without stopping to consider that Liza might be busy, she jumped up, ran across the room, and pulled the bell cord to the kitchen. She would ask Liza to find out.

Liza appeared at the door in just a few minutes, seemingly anxious to be of service to Mandie. "Miss 'Manda, you done fin'lly rung fo' me," she said as Mandie opened the door and stepped back for her to enter. "Now jes' tell me what you be wantin' and I'll git it."

"Liza, I'm sorry to bother you from your other work, but I was wondering if you could find out how my mother is this afternoon since I am not allowed to go anywhere near her room. I know you aren't allowed either, but I also know you have a way of finding things out," Mandie quickly told her.

"I sho' do, Missy 'Manda," Liza said with a big grin. "Be right back." She hurried out of the room and back down the corridor.

And Liza was right back. By the time Mandie had washed her face and hands, which she felt were dirty after her visit to the sooty depot, Liza was knocking on the door. Mandie opened the door and tried to decide from the expression on Liza's face what the report would be. She held her breath as she waited for the girl to speak.

"Well, things be de same, Missy 'Manda," Liza informed her. "She ain't no bettuh, but she ain't no worser neithuh." She looked at Mandie with a solemn expression as she entered the room.

Mandie blew out her breath and said, "Oh, Liza, I'm so thankful she's no worse. Now if Dr. Plumbley will only hurry and get here! I'm sure he'll know what to do."

"He done sent you dat message dat he would be heah an' I knows he will be heah soon," Liza told her. "Now I'll keep check on things and I'll let you know if anythin' change, one way or t'other. I promises."

"Thank you, Liza," Mandie said. "Are Uncle Ned and Morning Star still here?"

"Dey heah and he be he'pin' wid de wood fo' de cookstove and she be doin' things fo' Jenny in de kitchen," Liza explained.

"I wish there was something I could do. I feel so useless," Mandie said as she walked about her room.

"Now you got 'nuff to do worryin' 'bout yo' mama," Liza told her. "You jes' let everybody else worry 'bout de housework." She grinned big and added, "'Sides, some o' dem rich kinpeople done rolled up dey sleeves and pitched in to he'p. Why, one lady even baked a cake this mawnin'. I'se s'prised Jenny let huh git in huh kitchen. And Miz Cornwallis next do', she been sendin' heaps o' food ovuh."

"Polly's mother?" Mandie said as she stopped to listen to Liza. "Have you seen Polly around lately?"

"No, not aftuh I runs huh off," Liza said, shaking her head. "Doctuh son, he say he gwine outside fo' a walk and when he come back he say he saw huh in de yard and he tole huh to go home 'cause o' de fever."

"Did she go home?" Mandie asked. "Did Joe see that she went home?"

"I don't be knowin', Missy 'Manda," Liza said. "But he already wantin' to know kin he come up and talk to you agin. I said I let him know when you lets me know."

Mandie thought for a moment and then said, "Liza, when you see Joe, would you please tell him I might come downstairs later?"

"You is?" Liza asked in surprise. "You gwine down der 'mongst all dem nosey kinpeople?"

"Nosey kinpeople?" Mandie asked.

"Dey fo'ever askin' questions 'bout you, Missy 'Manda, one black-headed lady in partic'lar, a young one," Liza explained.

"Questions about me?" Mandie asked. "What kind of questions?"

"Dey mostly wantin' to know where you at, and when you gwine come downstairs so's dey kin see what you looks like," Liza said. "I keeps tellin' 'em you restin' and don't want to be disturbed wid their questions."

"I suppose I should go down and at least meet these people since they are kinpeople, but I figure they will all converge on me like a bunch of flies," Mandie said. "And I don't feel like being nice to people right now. And, Liza, when you tell Joe that I might come downstairs, please don't let anyone else hear you. I might decide not to go down there."

"I will be sho' nobody else knows," Liza told her.

"Oh, and Liza, if you happen to see Dr. Plumbley coming to the front door, or find out that he is here, please let me know at once. I still haven't talked to Dr. Woodard about him," Mandie said. "Dr. Plumbley might get here any time now."

"I keeps an eye out fo' him," Liza said. "Now I has to git back downstairs 'less you wants sumpin' else, Missy 'Manda."

"No, thank you, Liza. I'll see you later, either downstairs or up here," Mandie told her.

When Liza left, Mandie decided to go up and see if her grandmother planned to go downstairs. Her grandmother would know how to handle these "nosey kinpeople," as Liza called them. And she really would like to look them over and try to spot the owner of the voice who had been saying, "So you are Amanda." Then, too, there might be some clue as to who had been in the tunnel.

Mrs. Taft was preparing to go downstairs when Mandie knocked on her door.

"Come on in, dear, I was just fixing to descend among all those visitors downstairs," Mrs. Taft told her.

Mandie stepped inside the room and watched her grandmother freshen up her hairdo in front of the bureau mirror.

"Grandmother, I was thinking, maybe I ought to at least go down and meet these people. I understand they are all kinpeople," Mandie said, sitting on a chair nearby.

Mrs. Taft turned to look at her and said, "Yes, they are all kinpeople, but they're the kind you never see or hear from except at funerals."

Mandie quickly caught her breath and turned pale.

"I'm sorry, dear, I was referring to the funeral for your little brother, of course," Mrs. Taft said as she finished her hair.

"Are they your kinpeople, or my father's kinpeople?" Mandie asked.

"I believe all your Shaw kinpeople live a long way off and never come back here, and of course you know your Cherokee kinpeople on your grandmother's side," Mrs. Taft said thoughtfully. "I understand the people downstairs are mostly from your grandfather Taft's side of the family."

"Oh, I've never met any of them. In fact I don't even know anything about them," Mandie said. "I know I must have Taft relatives. But, Grandmother, what about your relatives? Don't you have any?" She stood up to walk around.

"My only brother died years ago, dear. He never married and therefore never had any children. And my mother and father both were only children in their families," Mrs. Taft explained. "I may have some very distant cousins somewhere. But you and your mother are really all I have. You see why you both are so precious to me?" She came to put an arm around Mandie.

Mandie hugged her back and said, "You are precious to me, too, Grandmother. I think I would like to meet these Taft kinpeople, though."

"Well, just come with me, dear, and you can get to know them," Mrs. Taft said as she opened the door.

Mandie hesitated as she said, "Grandmother, I don't want to stay long down there. I'm sure they'll ask questions and I'm not in a nice mood."

"I understand, dear. You just come on back upstairs when you get ready," Mrs. Taft said, leading the way into the corridor.

As they walked down the stairs, Mandie asked, "Do you know the latest word on my mother, Grandmother? Liza checked for me a little while ago and she was no better and no worse."

"I know, dear. I keep in touch with things every hour," Mrs. Taft said as she walked ahead of Mandie. "Have you heard anything else from Dr. Plumbley?"

"No, Grandmother, but I imagine he will be here any time now. I hope so, anyway," Mandie replied. "I went to the depot to check the train schedules from New York and, Grandmother, did you know they don't even go by a definite time for trains to arrive?"

Mrs. Taft stopped on the steps and looked back at Mandie as she asked, "You went to the train depot? Amanda, you could have gotten Abraham to do that."

"No, Grandmother, because no one else knows Dr. Plumbley is coming except for Liza," Mandie told her. She slowly added, "I haven't even talked to Dr. Woodard about him yet. In fact, I don't know how to catch up with Dr. Woodard without going to my mother's room, and that is forbidden."

"You just tell Liza to give him a message that you want to talk to him, dear," Mrs. Taft said, going on down the stairs. "In fact, why don't you just tell Joe to tell him for you?"

"Oh, no, Grandmother, that wouldn't ever do," Mandie quickly protested. "You see, I'm afraid Dr. Woodard might just get angry with me for having Dr. Plumbley come, and Joe probably would, too. I have to tell Dr. Woodard myself."

"Then you'd better do it soon or Dr. Plumbley will be here," her grandmother told her as they came to the bottom of the staircase on the first floor.

Mrs. Taft paused there and Mandie stayed beside her. She could hear voices murmuring nearby and she decided the kinpeople were in the parlor. Liza came into the hallway from the kitchen. She was carrying a tray, loaded with a silver teapot, chinaware, and teacakes. When she saw Mandie and Mrs. Taft, she stopped.

"Why, I'se glad y'all come down right now, Miz Taft, 'cause we be havin' tea in de parlor," Liza said. She went on down the hallway and into the parlor.

Mrs. Taft and Mandie followed. When they stopped in the doorway, the visitors in the room stopped talking to look at them. Mandie felt uncomfortable under their stare, and if her grandmother had not been with her she would have turned and fled.

Mrs. Taft walked on into the room. "I thought I'd better come down for a while and speak to y'all," she said. She sat down on a small settee. Mandie followed and sat beside her.

Mandie didn't listen to what her grandmother was saying to these people. She was busy looking each one over. They were mostly older women. A few young women sat together on one side of the room and several men were grouped together in the far corner. They were all wearing black, just as Liza and Joe had told her. She looked down at her gingham dress and then quickly glanced at her grandmother. Mrs. Taft was dressed in black, too. Mandie realized she should have changed her clothes, too, but her grandmother had not mentioned it.

An older woman with gray hair reached for the teapot on the tray that Liza had set on a table in front of her. She glanced at Mrs. Taft and quickly withdrew her hand. "I'm sorry, Mary Elizabeth," she said to Mrs. Taft. "I was going to pour the tea, but of course since you are here—"

"Go right ahead," Mrs. Taft interrupted her. "I don't really feel up to staying long anyway."

Mandie had never heard her grandmother called by her first name and it took a minute for her to realize the woman had addressed Mrs. Taft.

"Amanda," Mrs. Taft said. "This lady is your aunt Dorabelle Taft. She was married to your grandfather Taft's brother, Joseph, until he died many years ago." Mrs. Taft went on introducing other relatives around the huge room. They all looked prim, proper, and rich, Mandie thought, until Mrs. Taft came to the last one. She was sitting near the group of men and Mandie learned her name was Isabelle Evins, the daughter of Aunt Dorabelle.

"Isabelle is your mother's first cousin, dear," Mrs. Taft said. "They are almost exactly the same age."

Isabelle gave Mandie a big smile. Mandie thought she was beautiful, with thick black hair and eyes almost as blue as Mandie's. When Isabelle stood up to accept a cup of tea from her mother, Mandie noticed that she was thinner and taller than her own mother.

Mandie was suddenly aware of another young woman coming into the parlor. She was a duplicate of Isabelle, the same black hair, blue eyes, and smile.

"And, dear, this is Isabelle's sister, Emily," Mrs. Taft told Mandie.

"Twins?" Mandie whispered.

Mrs. Taft smiled at her and said in a low voice, "Emily is one year younger than Isabelle."

Mandie wondered if Emily was married. Isabelle was introduced as Isabelle Evins. Therefore, she must have a husband, but Mrs. Taft had not added a last name to Emily. She watched as Emily joined her sister and the nearby group of men immediately stood up, offering her a chair. Emily settled for a seat next to Isabelle.

Mandie decided she had not seen anyone in this room before. Of course she had only glimpsed the woman from behind who had entered the tunnel, but she couldn't picture any one of these as being that woman.

Mrs. Taft was carrying on a conversation with Aunt Dorabelle about the old days when both their husbands were living. Mandie tried to think up some way to escape these strangers. Finally she slipped out unnoticed and went to her room. She had too many worries to sit and listen to such talk.

Chapter 9 / Decision Regarding Elizabeth

Liza brought Mandie her supper on a tray that night. Mandie didn't leave her room again. And she was awake half the night as thoughts of her mother and her little brother whirled through her mind. Snowball didn't stay put on the foot of her bed either, but prowled around the room.

The next morning Mandie woke with a feeling of excitement. She felt her prayers for her mother were going to be answered. So when Liza came tapping on her door Mandie immediately wanted to know how her mother was.

She jumped out of bed and ran to the door. Snowball raced by her and into the hallway as she admitted Liza.

"Liza, please find out how my mother is doing," Mandie told the Negro girl.

"Why, I'se gwine do dat right now," Liza said, surprised at Mandie's exuberance. "But I also needs to know if'n you wants to eat heah or downstairs dis mawnin'."

"I'll just eat up here, if you don't mind, Liza, but first I have to know how my mother is," Mandie said.

"Be right back, Missy 'Manda," Liza said, turning to go down the hallway.

Mandie grabbed a dress from the chifferobe and quickly put it on. She felt an unexplained urgency that she be dressed and ready for whatever was about to happen. She quickly brushed out her long blonde hair and hastily plaited it.

By that time Liza had come back, and when she came into the room, Mandie practically held her breath until Liza spoke.

"She still hanging on, Missy 'Manda. Doctuh Woodard, he say no better, no worse, jes' like yesta'day," Liza reported.

"Thank the Lord," Mandie said as she grasped Liza's hand and squeezed it. "Liza, my mother is going to get well. I just feel it."

Liza put an arm around Mandie and said, "I knows she is. She got lots of things to do in this heah world yet."

Mandie leaned back and asked, "What do you mean, Liza?"

Liza smiled big, stepped back to look at Mandie, and said, "Well, de most important thing she gotta do is raise dis heah chile named 'Manda."

The girls laughed together. And the laughter made Mandie feel better.

"Now, what 'bout breakfus'?" Liza asked. "You don' wanta go downstairs? 'Cause dat doctuh son he done be in de kitchen wantin' to know if you'se comin' down."

At that moment Mrs. Taft appeared in the doorway. "Amanda, are you going downstairs for breakfast?" she asked.

Mandie looked at her for a moment and then asked, "Do I have to?"

"Why, no, dear," Mrs. Taft said, and then with a smile she added, "And I don't have to either." Turning to Liza she asked, "Would you mind bringing us a tray up here to Amanda's room?"

"Why, sho' 'nuff, Miz Taft," Liza said. "I be right back." She started down the hallway.

"Liza, wait," Mandie called to her. As Liza paused, Mandie asked her grandmother, "Do you mind if Joe eats with us up here? Liza said he's in the kitchen asking about me."

Mrs. Taft's eyes twinkled as she said, "Of course not, dear. Joe is good company."

Liza, listening from the hallway, called back, "Den I'se gwine bring dat doctuh son back wid de trays." She continued on her way.

As Mrs. Taft had said, Joe was good company. He kept asking questions about their European journey. He listened intently as Mrs. Taft described some of the places they had visited. And Mandie was drawn into the conversation.

As they talked, Mandie remembered those wonderful days when she had lived with her father at Charley Gap. Joe had always been her friend then. He had understood her sorrows. And after she had come to live with her uncle John, who married her mother after her father's death, Joe had kept flowers on her father's grave there on the mountaintop. She felt a lot of love for the boy.

When they had finished eating, Mrs. Taft told Mandie, "I'm going to my room to catch up on some correspondence. You need to get outside for fresh air and exercise, dear." She left the room.

"Yes, Grandmother, I will," Mandie called after her. She and Joe picked up the trays and carried them to the dumbwaiter.

"Let's go sit on the front porch," Joe suggested.

Mandie agreed. They left by the back entrance and

walked around to the front of the house. Joe led the way to the swing on the front porch.

"Seems like you were gone all summer when, in fact, you were only gone a few weeks," Joe told her as they sat down. "But I suppose you managed to cram a few adventures into that time." He smiled at her as he ran his long fingers through his unruly brown hair.

"Oh, we had lots of adventures," Mandie replied. "I wish you could have been with us." She stared into space as she remembered some of the mysteries they'd encountered.

"I'd like to go to Europe someday," Joe told her as he kept smiling. "Maybe you could go back and show me around."

Mandie smiled too. "I'd never be able to show you around," she said. "I'd get good and lost. And I'm not sure I want to go back again. My grandmother mentioned sending me to school over there, but I certainly don't want to do that."

"I hope you don't go away like that," Joe said with a slight frown.

"I won't. I refuse," Mandie said as she suddenly pushed the swing into motion. "Joe, do you think there was someone in the tunnel when we were? Remember that noise when your lantern went out?"

"It sounded like a door creaking open, or closing, but then that could have been just the subfloor in the house settling," he said.

"But I don't believe we were under the house when that happened," Mandie said. "We must have been far enough down the tunnel to be under the ground."

"I suppose the overhead of the tunnel was built with rafters, and they could have made the noise," he said.

Mandie gasped as she slowed the swing with her foot.

"Do you think the tunnel is dangerous? That it's sinking or something?" she asked.

"Since that tunnel has been there for probably sixty-something years, I don't imagine it's going to cave in now," Joe assured her. "But you know, wood shrinks and expands according to the weather, and that could cause some of the structure to squeak."

"Maybe I ought to ask Uncle John if he has ever had it inspected for safety," she suggested. "I don't think anyone ever goes in there, except us, and it could deteriorate without anyone noticing."

"He probably keeps check on it," Joe said. "You know, Mandie, you really ought to think of a use for that tunnel."

"Like what? It's all dark and spooky and not really good for anything," Mandie said.

"We need to think about that. It was very useful to the Cherokees when your great-grandfather built it, and there must be some purpose for it now," he said.

"Well, let me know if you think up anything," Mandie said. "Why don't we go look at the exit in the woods and see if it's still closed?"

"A walk wouldn't hurt us," Joe agreed as they both stood up. "I saw Polly down there yesterday. She said she was watching the exit. When I asked her what for, she said you wanted her to." He looked down at Mandie as they walked down the porch steps into the yard.

Mandie laughed slightly. "I was only trying to get rid of her," she said. "She came up to my room and—"

Joe interrupted, "She came up to your room? My father has forbidden her to come into the house because of the fever. I hope she doesn't catch it."

"I've warned her, too, but you know Polly. You can't make her do anything she doesn't want to do," Mandie said.

Mandie and Joe walked through the woods behind

the house and down the hill to the tunnel exit. There was no one in sight. As they pushed through the bushes to check the opening, they suddenly came face-to-face with Polly. She was leaning against the doorframe.

Polly immediately rushed at Mandie. "You told me you weren't coming back down here. And Joe ran me off when he found me here yesterday," she said with a deep frown.

"I didn't plan on coming down here again anytime soon, but I changed my mind," Mandie told her. She reached around Polly and tried the door handle. It was locked.

"Polly, you really ought to go home and stay away from here until we get rid of the fever in the house," Joe cautioned her.

Polly stomped her foot and scowled at the two. "I am going home and I won't be back. Next time you want a favor for anything, don't ask me," she told Mandie as she ran off through the woods.

"I'm sorry," Mandie called after her.

"Well!" Joe said, watching Polly leave. Then he looked at the door and said, "It's locked. Let's go back to the house."

The two young people took their time strolling through the woods and on into the flower garden at one side of the house.

"Let's sit in the summerhouse," Mandie suggested.

"Good idea. From there we can see most of what's going on," Joe agreed.

Just as they reached the structure in the yard, Mandie heard a horse coming down the road. She stopped to look. As it came nearer she realized it was a hired carriage from the train depot. Without waiting to see whether it stopped before her house or not she began running toward the front gate.

"Mandie, what's wrong?" Joe called as he hurried after her.

"It's Dr. Plumbley! It's Dr. Plumbley!" she cried, excitedly jumping up and down as the driver stopped at the hitching post.

A huge Negro man in fine dress stepped down from the vehicle. The driver unloaded several black medical bags and a small trunk. Dr. Plumbley did not see Mandie until she yelled to him as she neared the gate in the white fence.

"Dr. Plumbley! Dr. Plumbley!" she cried, opening the gate and grabbing the doctor's large hands. "Oh, thank you! Thank you!"

Joe stood by, watching and seemingly puzzled.

"This is Dr. Plumbley, remember him?" Mandie said to Joe.

"Yes, sir," Joe said, stepping forward to shake hands with the man.

Dr. Plumbley smiled and patted Joe on the back. "I do believe you are getting tall."

"Yes, sir, one day I'll probably be as tall as you are," Joe agreed, straightening his thin shoulders. He bent to pick up two bags and said, "Let me help you take these to the house."

"That's kind of you. I'll get these others, and the driver will bring the trunk," Dr. Plumbley said as he lifted two bags and tucked another one under his arm.

Mandie was speechless with happiness as she led the way up the walkway to the front door. Liza was standing there, evidently having seen Dr. Plumbley arrive. They greeted each other and then Liza tugged at Mandie's sleeve to hold her back a moment as Joe and Dr. Plumbley went into the front hall.

"Missy 'Manda, has you done tole de doctuh man

upstairs dat dis heah doctuh be comin'?" Liza anxiously whispered to Mandie.

Mandie felt a stab in her stomach. She had not even thought about the meeting of the two doctors since she had talked to her grandmother about Dr. Plumbley. "Not yet," she whispered to Liza.

By that time Mrs. Taft had appeared in the front hallway. She quickly stepped forward. "Dr. Plumbley, you are so kind to come. I believe Liza has a room ready for you." She looked at Liza who nodded in the affirmative.

"Right dis way, doctuh," Liza told him, going to the bottom of the staircase.

"Thank you, Mrs. Taft. I'll see you again shortly," Dr. Plumbley said as he followed Liza.

"I'll bring these bags on up," Joe told him, and he followed Dr. Plumbley.

As soon as they were out of sight up the staircase, Mandie whispered to her grandmother, "Grandmother, I haven't told Dr. Woodard. What will I do? What's going to happen now?"

"Don't worry, dear. I'm sure everything will be all right," Mrs. Taft told her.

"I don't know, Grandmother. I feel so awful about this," Mandie insisted.

"You should feel good about asking Dr. Plumbley to come. I'm sure he will know what to do to help your mother, and that's all that counts. Personal feelings shouldn't be allowed to affect what you have done," Mrs. Taft assured her. "But you really should have told Dr. Woodard."

Joe came bounding down the staircase and stopped when he saw them still in the hallway.

"Evidently y'all were expecting Dr. Plumbley. Has he come to take over your mother's case, Mandie?" Joe asked stiffly.

Before Mandie could answer, Mrs. Taft said, "Yes, we knew he was coming. Remember the old saying. Two heads are better than one. But it will be strictly up to your father whether he wants Dr. Plumbley on Mandie's mother's case."

Joe looked directly at Mandie, whose nervous hands were plunged deep in her gingham pockets. "Why didn't you tell me he was coming?"

"I—I'm sorry, Joe," Mandie said in a shaky voice. Her eyes filled with tears and she ran past him up the steps.

"Joe, please be patient with Amanda. She has almost more than she can bear right now," Mandie heard her grandmother saying.

"Yes, ma'am," came Joe's answer.

Mandie ran into her room and slammed the door shut behind her with such force that it bounced partly open without her noticing. She sank into a big chair and put her head on the arm.

"I've acted so stupid," she scolded herself aloud. "Now Joe's angry with me and his father probably will be, too. I had all this time to tell Dr. Woodard and I kept putting it off."

Snowball wandered in from the hallway and jumped into the chair with his mistress. She paid no attention to him until he managed to get near her ear and began purring loudly. Then she moved enough to cuddle him in her arms.

Finally she sat up, dried her eyes, and said, "Other people's feelings, including mine, are not important. My mother is what matters." Snowball jumped down and ran out of the room.

"Dat's right, Missy 'Manda," Liza declared from the doorway. Mandie had not heard her come up. She was carrying a small tray with a teapot, sweet rolls, and cups on it. She went straight to a table nearby and set it down.

"What have you got, Liza?" Mandie asked, watching her.

"I has a cup o' tea fo' you and anybody else what happens by," Liza said. "Morning Star made dis heah concoction special fo' you. Dat means you gotta drink it." She placed a cup on a saucer, filled it with tea, and handed it to Mandie.

Mandie smelled the aroma and said with a smile, "This is mint tea, Liza. I've had it at Morning Star's house. The Cherokees claim it will cure anything." She took a sip. "Umm! It's delicious. Why don't you try some? There's another cup."

Liza shook her head. "No, thank you, Missy 'Manda," she said. "I ain't got nuthin' that be needin' curin'. You jes' drink it all." She moved around the room, plumping up pillows, straightening scarves on the tables, and she gave the bedspread a tug.

Mandie frowned as she watched her. "Liza, what are you doing? You've already straightened up my room one time today," she said.

"I knows dat, Missy 'Manda, but you cain't ever tell when you might git comp'ny," Liza said, straightening a fold in one of the draperies.

Mandie looked sternly at the girl and asked, "Liza, who is coming? Tell me this instant."

"I don' rightly be knowin'," Liza said, sauntering around the room.

"What are you up to?" Mandie demanded, placing the teacup back on the tray.

"Now, Missy 'Manda, you go drink dat tea. It be good fo' you," Liza said as she watched Mandie.

"Liza, you don't have to beg me to drink the tea. It is delicious," Mandie said. "I want to know what you're up to."

"Missy 'Manda, I ain't up to nuthin'," Liza said as she stopped to look at Mandie. "It be dat Injun man. He say Morning Star say fo' me to stay wid you till you drinks de tea. Now dat's all."

Mandie smiled and said, "Well, you can go now, because I am going to drink the tea." She picked up her cup and drank some more.

"Missy 'Manda, don' you wants to know what's goin' on?" Liza asked.

"I know what's going on," Mandie said with a sigh. "By this time Dr. Plumbley has found Dr. Woodard and Dr. Woodard is awfully angry with me for calling in another doctor without consulting him. And that means that Joe is also mad at me." She paused for a second. "I just hope Dr. Plumbley can help my mother. That's all that really matters."

"You don' really knows what's goin' on," Liza told her. "And I don' neithuh, 'cause Miz Taft, she sent me to de kitchen to git de tea fo' you. And when I come back out o' de kitchen ain't no sign o' nobody 'cept dem nosey kinpeople in de parlor."

Mandie sighed and looked at Liza. "You know, this is really a silly conversation. You don't know anything and I don't either," she said. "So, Liza, why don't you go roaming around and find out what's happening, then come back and tell me?"

Liza's eyes opened wide. "You really wants me to do dat?" and when Mandie nodded her head, she added, "All right den. Be right back."

Mandie sat there and drank the mint tea. She thought about the angel—she was sure it was an angel who had come to her room. Then the sudden knowledge had come that she must send for Dr. Plumbley. She was sure she had done the right thing, up to the point when she should have told Dr. Woodard.

A sudden tapping on the open door drew her attention and she looked up to see Dr. Plumbley and Dr. Woodard standing in her doorway. She stood up, flustered with not knowing what was about to be said.

"Come on in. I have plenty of chairs in here," Mandie told them and motioned to the chairs.

"Thank you, but we don't have time to sit down, Miss Amanda," Dr. Woodard told her. "Dr. Plumbley here has brought some new medicine with him from New York and we wanted to let you know that we're going to give it to your mother. We hope it will bring her out of the fever."

Mandie listened, her eyes growing wide. Dr. Woodard didn't seem to be angry with her. "Dr. Woodard, I apologize for not letting you know Dr. Plumbley was coming," she blurted out.

"Apologize? I think you should have told me, but you have done something wonderful for your mother and me. Dr. Plumbley has gotten far ahead of me in medicine. He's up there where he can learn about the latest developments, and I hope he can help your mother," Dr. Woodard said. "I'm thankful he could come."

"I'm going to use every bit of knowledge I have, Missy," Dr. Plumbley added. "We've had a lot of success with this medicine in New York lately."

Tears of happiness filled her blue eyes and she said in a shaky voice, "Oh, I thank you both. My mother is going to get well. I know she is."

"Your uncle John thinks so, too, Miss Amanda," Dr. Woodard said. "He said he had a dream or a vision the other night that bolstered his hopes. Your mother has been awfully sick, of course, but there is always hope until the last breath, because only the Lord knows when our days will end."

"I know, Dr. Woodard," Mandie said, rushing up to hug the old man's neck and then quickly backing off as she caught sight of Joe in the hallway.

Dr. Woodard turned to look behind him to see what Mandie had seen. Upon seeing Joe he smiled and said, "We've got work to do now. We have to be going. Just remember to keep praying."

"Oh, I will, Dr. Woodard. And, Dr. Plumbley, I thank you for dropping everything in New York and coming down here," Mandie said.

"I was actually on a few days' vacation when I received your wire. Therefore, you didn't interrupt anything important," Dr. Plumbley assured her.

The two doctors went on down the hallway and Joe came to stand in the doorway. He glanced at the tray on the table and asked, "Food?"

"No, it's tea. Come on in and have some," Mandie told him. "It's mint tea that Morning Star made."

Joe left the door open and came to sit by the table. Mandie poured him a cup of tea and handed it to him.

At that moment Liza came hurrying up to the doorway. She saw Joe and stopped outside.

"Joe, thanks for not getting mad at me for sending for Dr. Plumbley," Mandie said as she took her cup and they sat down.

"I wasn't mad. I was surprised because you usually tell me everything that goes on," Joe said with a big smile.

"Well, I didn't this time," Mandie said, smiling back. "But I promise to do better next time."

Liza, unseen, went on down the hallway.

Chapter 10 / Tears

Mandie knew Dr. Plumbley couldn't perform a miracle, but time dragged as he doctored her mother. Every day she hoped the fever would break, but Elizabeth remained the same.

Finally Dr. Plumbley told Mandie that her mother had several other things wrong with her besides the fever, and he began additional medication for those.

The visiting relatives held regular prayer meetings in the parlor, while Mandie, Uncle Ned, Mrs. Taft, and Joe had their own sessions.

Liza came to wake Mandie one morning with the news that Uncle John had asked her to get help to clear out a small parlor on the second floor and make the room into a dining room just for Mandie, Mrs. Taft, and whoever they wished to eat with them.

"I jes' wanted to let you know dat Mistuh John, he say fo' me to git dat parlor cleared out and make it a eatin' room fo' you and yo' grandma since y'all don't ever be

125

wantin' to dine wid dem nosey kinpeople," Liza told Mandie as she opened the draperies.

Mandie had gotten up to answer Liza's knock and now she reached for clothes to put on.

"I suppose that will be easier for you, even though we don't eat that much. You still have to carry trays though," Mandie said as she pulled a red gingham dress over her head.

"No, no, Missy 'Manda," Liza said as she straightened the bed. "Dis parlor be de one right next to de dumbwaiter, so all I has to do is move de food from de dumbwaiter to de table in de room. And I kin keep de clean dishes an' sech in de parlor room."

"Then that will be a lot better for us all," Mandie said as she buttoned the dress. "You know, Liza, I haven't had a chance to talk to my uncle John since I came home because he stays right with my mother. I imagine he's plumb worn out by now."

"Oh, he plumb wore out, but he rests on de settee in yo' mama's sittin' room," Liza explained. "And he leaves de door open so he kin see huh. Now Aunt Lou and de doctuhs, dey take turns sleepin' in de room on t'other side o' yo' mama's room."

"This has been a long ordeal for all of us," Mandie said as she buttoned her shoes.

"But it gwine end soon. You jes' wait an' see," Liza said in a hopeful voice. "And it gwine end real good, too."

"I hope and pray it will, Liza," Mandie said.

"Now, what you gwine do 'bout breakfus'? Yo' grandma comin' down heah to eat?" Liza asked.

"I suppose so, since she has been doing that just about ever since I came home," Mandie said. "And if you see Joe, please tell him about the room and say that he is welcome to eat with us—every meal if he wants to."

"I'll sho' let him know," Liza said. "In fact, he be de one I'se gwine ask to move de stuff out o' dat parlor. Now I go git de breakfus' and hope yo' grandma git heah in time."

"I'll run upstairs and tell her," Mandie said as she quickly plaited her long blonde hair.

Liza went for the food and Mandie climbed the steps to her grandmother's room. She knocked and knocked on the door and then pushed it far enough open to see inside. Mrs. Taft was not in the sitting room so Mandie looked into the bedroom. She wasn't there either.

"It's so early in the morning, I wonder where she could be," Mandie said to herself. "I'll go back to my room and wait. Maybe she'll come back by the time Liza gets our breakfast."

Mandie went back to her room, left the door open, and sat down near the table where Liza always put their food. In a few minutes Joe showed up at the doorway.

With a big smile, he said, "I got your message. Thanks a whole lot."

"Come on in and sit down," Mandie invited. "I know you don't like eating with those strangers downstairs and my grandmother always enjoys your company. I thought you might like to join us."

"Is your grandmother the only one who enjoys my company?" Joe teased.

Mandie felt herself blush, so she didn't dare look Joe straight in the eye. "Oh, Joe, you know I appreciate having you for a friend. We've been friends as long as I can remember," she said. "In fact, you and your father are like kinpeople."

"Well, thanks a lot," Joe said with a frown. "I distinctly remember the day your mother married your uncle John and you promised to marry me when we grow up—if I would get your father's house in Swain County back for you, and I certainly plan on doing that. I hope you are planning to keep your end of the bargain." He looked serious.

"Well, Joe, we have to grow up first and we don't know what will happen before then," Mandie said solemnly. "Why don't you ask me again when I am about eighteen?"

"I can guarantee you I will," Joe said. "In the meantime let me know if you change your mind."

"Change my mind?" Mandie asked.

"You know, like you said, if something happens that changes things between us," Joe replied. "And since I am a couple of years older than you are, by the time you become eighteen I will be on my way toward a career. I still plan on becoming a lawyer."

"You will make a wonderful lawyer, Joe, because you adhere to rules better than I do," Mandie said with a smile.

"Unless you manage to drag me along with you when you get involved in things that you shouldn't," Joe said, smiling back.

"Like the noise we heard in the tunnel?" Mandie asked. "I still think there was someone in there when we were."

"Well, it's too late to find out who it was. If you thought that, we should have looked around while we were there," Joe reminded her.

"Oh, Joe, you know how it works sometimes," Mandie argued. "After something suspicious happens, there is usually another occurrence or clue that can be worked back to the first event to solve the whole thing."

"Mandie, you should be a detective when you grow up," Joe teased with a big grin.

"No, that wouldn't be interesting," Mandie said. "It's just things that happen around me that I get interested in."

Joe suddenly stood up and said, "I forgot. I am supposed to go back to the kitchen to help Liza bring the trays to the dumbwaiter down there. Be right back."

Joe hurried out into the hallway and disappeared from Mandie's view.

"I wonder where my grandmother is?" Mandie said aloud to herself as she watched the hallway outside her door. "Surely she is not having breakfast downstairs."

She decided to run back upstairs and check her grandmother's room again. Mrs. Taft didn't have to pass Mandie's door to go up the flight to the third floor, and she might have returned to her room by now.

But when Mandie checked the sitting room and the bedroom, there was still no sign of her grandmother. She came back down the hallway, and as she passed one of the guest bedrooms, the sound of crying met her ears. The door was slightly open and Mandie, surprised, stopped to listen.

The crying continued, evidently muffled by a handkerchief, and Mandie decided to peek in to see who it was. She quietly pushed the door open enough to look inside the room. One of Aunt Dorabelle's daughters was sitting in a big chair near a window. Her head was bowed in her arms and Mandie couldn't see her face, but since the woman had black hair and was thin Mandie decided it had to be either Isabelle or Emily, but she couldn't determine which.

The woman in the room suddenly hushed, cleared her throat, and sniffed loudly. Mandie quickly stepped back and pulled the door closed. It appeared the woman was preparing to get up from the chair where she was sitting and Mandie didn't want to be seen.

I'll just hide, Mandie decided. She quickly looked at the row of doors down the hallway. They all seemed to be closed and Mandie didn't know whether the occupants were in the rooms or not, but she'd take a chance. Rushing down to the first door, she listened for a second, heard nothing, then quietly opened the door and slipped inside. She glanced around to be sure no one was there.

I just have to see who that was, Mandie thought. She opened the door just enough to see into the corridor.

In a few minutes Mandie heard a door open, and then the woman who had been crying came hurrying by the door where Mandie was watching. But the woman had put on a wide-brimmed bonnet and Mandie couldn't see her face as she went by.

"Oh, shucks!" Mandie said quietly. She softly slipped out into the hallway to watch the woman. Whoever she was, she went on toward the staircase and Mandie followed at a distance.

The woman was too quick for her, though. By the time Mandie had gotten to the second floor the woman was nowhere in sight. Mandie stood there looking around and finally went back to her own room.

Almost immediately Liza and Joe came in with the breakfast trays. Liza went back to the dumbwaiter and brought in the third tray.

"I don't know where my grandmother is," Mandie told Joe and Liza. "I don't know whether she'll get here in time to eat or not."

"Jus' keep de tray covered, Missy 'Manda. It'll stay warm," Liza said as she left the room to go back to her duties.

"Smells good," Joe said, lifting the cover from his tray.

"Yes, it does," Mandie agreed as she looked to see what she had.

At that moment Mrs. Taft came rushing into the room and went straight to Mandie. Her eyes were red from crying and she could barely speak as she hugged Mandie. Mandie's heart did flipflops. What was wrong?

"Grandmother, what is it?" Mandie asked as Mrs. Taft squeezed her tight.

Joe got to his feet and looked on.

"Amanda," Mrs. Taft was finally able to say. "The fever—broke—"

Mandie squeezed her grandmother back. "Oh, Grandmother! My mother is going to get well!" She pulled away from her grandmother's embrace and rushed to hug Joe.

Joe put his arms around Mandie and said, "Hey, don't cry about it. This is something to be happy about."

Mandie wiped her tears with the backs of her hands as she smiled at Joe and then at her grandmother, who had sat down. "I know it is. But I'm so happy I can't help crying!" she said, her voice trembling. She looked upward and said, "Thank you, dear God. Thank you."

"Yes, dear," Mrs. Taft managed to say as she used her handkerchief on her eyes. "I've never been so happy in my life!"

Mandie went to sit on the arm of her grandmother's chair. "Were you in there with my mother, Grandmother?" Mandie asked.

"No, dear, none of us can go in. Your mother will be moved to another room now and her room will be fumigated to kill the fever germs," Mrs. Taft explained. "Dr. Woodard came knocking on my door about dawn this morning and asked me to come downstairs and wait outside Elizabeth's room. He left before I could ask questions and I was so upset I almost never got my clothes on. Then when I got down there the door was open and Dr. Woodard was waiting for me in the hallway." She stopped for breath.

"Did you see my mother?" Mandie asked.

"Yes, dear, I could see her from the hallway. She was propped up on pillows and her eyes were open. I'm sure she saw me, but Dr. Woodard said she was too weak to move or talk right now. It's going to be a long time before she completely recovers her strength."

Joe had been listening and now he said, "Mandie, you did the right thing when you sent for Dr. Plumbley. Evidently the medicine he brought with him worked. And now my father will know more about what to do with other patients who may get the fever."

"I appreciate your saying that, Joe, but it wasn't entirely my decision to send for Dr. Plumbley," Mandie said.

Joe quickly looked at her and asked, "It wasn't?"

"I'll explain one day when we have time to talk for a while," Mandie promised. She didn't know how Joe would react to her story about the angel in her room. And she had not talked about this to her grandmother either. It was something so personal and dear to her heart that she couldn't discuss it. But she was sure her mother was healed because of the angel's visit.

Liza appeared in the doorway with a big grin on her face. She ran to Mandie, hugged her, and danced around the room. "Hallelujah! I done tole you, Missy 'Manda, it would all end soon, and real good, too, and it did. De Lawd done answered all our prayers."

Mandie glanced up to see Uncle Ned coming through the doorway. He also had a big smile on his wrinkled old face. She ran to him and he bent to embrace her. "Big God answer our prayers," he said.

"Oh, yes, yes!" Mandie said excitedly.

"Now we thank Big God," the old Indian said. He knelt in the middle of the floor and Mrs. Taft, Mandie, Joe, and Liza all followed without hesitation. Looking upward, Uncle Ned said, "We thank Big God. Make Papoose's mother well soon. Only Big God do this. We thank you."

The others followed with their own thanks, and when they rose from the floor tears were in all their eyes, tears of happiness.

Liza glanced at the trays on the table and said, "Y'all ain't eat no breakfus' yet. It gittin' cold."

"Oh, I forgot," Mandie said. Looking at Uncle Ned she asked, "Have you had breakfast yet?"

"By break of day Morning Star cooked breakfast for her and me," he said. "Must go now. Chop wood."

"I'll be down to help as soon as I eat, Uncle Ned," Joe promised as he sat down at his tray. "I won't be long."

Uncle Ned smiled and left the room.

"I gotta git goin', too," Liza said. "We'se gittin' 'nuther room ready fo' yo' mama, Missy 'Manda. I'll let you know when she's moved."

"Oh, please do, Liza," Mandie said quickly, her eyes shining with happiness.

Liza left and Mrs. Taft, Joe, and Mandie began to eat their breakfast.

"I'm so happy, it's hard to swallow anything," Mandie said, her hand flitting from one thing to another on her tray.

"You have to eat, dear, to keep yourself well. It's a blessing that no one else has caught the fever," Mrs. Taft said.

"Yes, my father was worried about everybody else in this house," Joe agreed.

As soon as they were all finished, Mrs. Taft wanted to go to her room.

"I must get back upstairs and make myself present-able," Mrs. Taft said, looking down at her clothes. "And if you hear that Elizabeth has been moved, Amanda, please let me know."

"And you, too, Grandmother. I may be the last one to know," Mandie said as she and Joe picked up the trays.

Mrs. Taft left and Mandie and Joe carried the trays to the dumbwaiter. Then they went back to Mandie's room to sit down.

Suddenly Mandie's face clouded over as she said, "If only Dr. Plumbley could have come sooner and doctored Samuel with his new medicine."

Joe spoke sharply, "Mandie, you've got to believe me that Samuel had lots of other problems. He would not have survived to be much older, anyway. Please get that through your head."

Mandie gave Joe an angry look as she pursed her lips and got up to walk around the room. *I wish he would stop telling me that,* she thought to herself. *I know it's all a lie. I also know God took Samuel to punish me for not loving him as I should have.*

"I'm sorry, Mandie," Joe said, quietly watching her.

Mandie whirled around and looked at him. She wasn't going to discuss this any further. Searching for something to say to change the subject she said, "I found a woman crying in a bedroom upstairs this morning."

"A woman crying in a bedroom upstairs?" Joe repeated. "Well, what was that all about?"

Mandie came to sit down again. "I went upstairs to get my grandmother to come to breakfast down here and she wasn't there," she said. "As I walked down the hallway I heard someone crying and I peeked in the door to see who it was. I'm sure it was one of Aunt Dorabelle's daughters. I couldn't see her face, but it looked like one of them."

"Then what happened?" Joe asked as he continued watching Mandie.

"She left the room and I had to hurry to get inside another room before she saw me. I watched through a crack in the door to see her pass, but she had put on a bonnet and I couldn't see her face," Mandie explained. "I'd just like to know what she was crying about."

"Mandie, that's none of your business. You shouldn't go around spying on people," Joe said sharply.

"Oh, Joe Woodard, I was not spying. I thought maybe I could help her or something if I knew what was wrong," Mandie replied with a deep frown.

"Well, evidently she quit crying enough to leave the room," Joe said.

"Yes, and I'd like to know who she was, too," Mandie said.

"You might as well quit worrying about it because it's too late now to find out who she was," Joe said.

"No, it isn't. I'll ask Liza who is using that room," Mandie said.

"And what good will that do you?" Joe asked.

"At least I'll know," Mandie said.

"I imagine all your kinpeople will go home now that your mother is recovering," Joe remarked. "So you don't need to get involved in anything concerning them."

"Oh, Joe," Mandie said, getting up again to walk around the room. "Sometimes you just don't understand."

Joe rose from the chair and caught Mandie's hand as she came near him.

"I'm sorry, Mandie. I know you're all wound up with the exciting news about your mother and that you just aren't thinking right about everything now," he said gently.

Liza appeared in the doorway. She spoke to Joe and said, "Mistuh John, he say nevah mine 'bout cleanin' out de parlor room now. Comp'ny leavin' soon and things git back to normal-like."

Joe smiled at her and said, "That's fine, Liza, but if you do need me, let me know." Turning back to Mandie, he said, "I promised to help Uncle Ned. I'll catch up with you later."

"All right," Mandie agreed.

Joe walked down the hallway with Liza.

Mandie began wondering when she'd be able to see her mother. She was anxiously counting the minutes. She deeply loved her mother and, now that the fever had gone, she felt as though she were floating on clouds. Soon she'd be able to talk to her and tell her how much she loved her.

Then a sudden thought hit her and she flopped into a nearby chair. Did her mother know that Samuel had died, or had that happened after her mother got so desperately ill? If she knew, what would she have to say about it?

"Please, dear Lord, don't let my mother get angry with me," Mandie said. "She knows how I treated Samuel when he was born."

She was anxious to see her mother, but in another way she dreaded it.

Chapter 11 / Changes

Mandie didn't budge from her room all morning for fear someone would come to tell her that she could see her mother, and she wouldn't be there.

No one came to visit her while she waited and her thoughts roamed. Who was the woman she'd seen crying? Was it Isabelle or Emily? What was wrong that would make a grown woman cry like that? And where did she go?

Then her mind flitted off to the mystery of the woman she had seen enter the tunnel. Was she one of the kinpeople visiting the family? Or was she an outsider who somehow had gotten into the house? Not only that, where did she get the keys? Mr. Jason had said he had not let anyone have the keys to Uncle John's library door or the tunnel.

And what would she say to her mother when she finally got to see her? She needed to find out whether her mother knew little Samuel was gone. She remembered Polly telling her that Uncle John had wired her grandmother about Samuel and that her mother had become sick with the fever while they were on the way home. In that case, her mother would know about Samuel. But Mandie knew she couldn't always believe Polly. Sometimes she got the truth mixed up, and sometimes it seemed to be on purpose. She needed to talk to her grandmother.

"Oh, there are so many unanswered questions!" Mandie exclaimed aloud.

And had she imagined the voice that said, "So you are Amanda," or was the voice real? If so, whose voice was it? And where was she now?

"I'm beginning to doubt my own mind," Mandie told herself.

Snowball came into the room through the open door and rubbed around Mandie's ankles. When she paid him no attention, he jumped up on the big bed. After washing his face, he curled up and went to sleep.

Liza brought Mandie out of her reverie. "Eatin' time, Missy 'Manda," she said from the doorway. "Guess you be eatin' up heah?"

Mandie blinked her eyes back into focus and said, "If you don't mind, Liza. I'm afraid to leave my room because someone is supposed to let me know when I can see my mother."

"Dat other room is done clean spotless. All dey got left to do is pick Miz 'Lizbeth up and put huh in dat nice clean bed," Liza said with a big smile. "And I knows it be clean 'cause I done it."

"Then it won't be long before I can see her, will it?" Mandie asked, eagerly waiting for Liza's reply.

"I don't be knowin' 'bout dat, Missy 'Manda," Liza said.

Mandie suddenly realized Liza could probably answer one question for her. "Liza, you've been here all the time," she began. "Did Samuel . . . does my mother know Samuel is . . . gone?"

"She sho' does, Missy 'Manda. He got de fever first

and she held him night an' day an' all de time Doctuh Woodard say she ought not to," Liza said with a sad expression. "She say she cain't stand to see him suffer. So she has to hold him an' he die right there in huh arms."

Mandie listened with tears in her eyes. "He did?" was all she could say.

"And when he die, Miz 'Lizbeth pass plumb out and she ain't be back wid us till today," Liza explained.

Mandie couldn't speak for a few minutes. Liza stood there quietly, apparently understanding Mandie's grief.

Finally Liza said, "I go git de trays now, Missy 'Manda. Doctuh son, he be wantin' to come eat wid you. An' yo' grandmother, where she be? She gwine eat here too?"

"I suppose you might as well bring their trays in here, too," Mandie said.

"Yes, please do, Liza," Mrs. Taft spoke from the doorway. Neither one of the girls had seen her walk up. She came on into the room and sat down.

"Yessum, Miz Taft. I go git de food," Liza said, and went off down the corridor.

"Any word, Grandmother, when we can see my mother?" Mandie asked anxiously.

"No, dear, I've been in my room waiting, and I knew it was time to eat so I came down here to join you," Mrs. Taft said. "I hate to bother the doctors, but maybe I should go see what I can find out."

"Liza just told me the other room is ready for my mother to be moved to, so it won't be long now," Mandie told her.

"Well, they ought to let us know something," Mrs. Taft said.

Liza returned with the trays and with Joe.

"Any news from your father, Joe?" Mrs. Taft quickly asked as they settled down to eat after Liza had left the room.

"No, ma'am, I haven't even seen him. I suppose he'll

let you know first when they get Mandie's mother moved," Joe said as he devoured a hot biscuit.

Dr. Woodard did let them know first. When they had just finished eating and Mandie and Joe were preparing to take the trays to the dumb waiter, Dr. Woodard came to Mandie's room in search of Mrs. Taft and Mandie.

"I'm glad I caught you two together so I only have to make one little speech," Dr. Woodard said as he stood in the doorway.

"A speech?" Mandie asked.

"Yes, now you can both see Elizabeth, on certain conditions," he began. "She has been awfully sick, as you both know, and therefore, she is awfully weak. I'm asking that you not touch her, not only for her sake but because we doctors are not sure about when the fever germ leaves a patient. Therefore, it would be best for all concerned if you would only stand in the doorway and speak to her. And that should be limited to a half dozen words."

Mandie was listening and she asked, "My mother is going to get well, isn't she, Dr. Woodard?"

"Yes, Miss Amanda, I would say she will, given the proper attention and care," Dr. Woodard replied. "But you've got to understand she is not going to get well overnight. We can only gradually bring her back to normal health."

"We understand, Dr. Woodard," Mrs. Taft said. "Now may we go visit her?"

"Yes, ma'am, that's what I came here for, to tell you she has been moved into a clean room and that you can see her now," the doctor replied.

"Mandie, you won't be gone long. Should I wait outside on the window seat for you?" Joe asked. "And I'll take care of the trays."

Mrs. Taft was hurrying out the doorway behind Dr. Woodard and Mandie rushed to catch up with her as she called back to Joe, "All right. I'll be back soon."

Dr. Woodard led them to a room in the same wing as Elizabeth's own room and stopped at a door not far from it. He slowly opened the door, stepped inside, and looked back at Mandie and her grandmother.

Mandie quickly looked in at her mother. She was wearing a frilly nightgown and was propped up on some pillows. As Dr. Woodard opened the door, Elizabeth turned to look at him. When her eyes caught sight of Mandie and Mrs. Taft in the doorway, she tried to raise herself up off the pillows as they stopped in the doorway.

"My darling!" she whispered weakly. "And Mother."

Mandie had all she could do to keep from running to her. "Mother, I love you. I love you."

"Elizabeth, I love you, too," Mrs. Taft said in a shaky voice.

Elizabeth seemed unable to speak anymore. Dr. Woodard motioned for Mandie and Mrs. Taft to leave.

"We'll be back, Mother," Mandie called to her.

"Love," Elizabeth managed to say as they turned to walk down the hallway, and Dr. Woodard closed the door.

"I'm so happy I just can't stand it!" Mandie said as they went toward her room.

"So am I, dear, and you know what? We forgot to ask Dr. Woodard when we could come back," Mrs. Taft said.

Mandie stopped in the hallway and said, "Maybe I should go back and ask him." She looked back and saw Dr. Plumbley hurrying to catch up with them. "Here comes Dr. Plumbley, Grandmother."

They waited for him. Mandie immediately grabbed his big, strong hands and, looking up at him, said, "Oh, Dr. Plumbley, you saved my mother's life. I'm so thankful!"

"Now wait a minute, Missy," the doctor protested. "I didn't save your mother's life. Only God could do that. I merely used the knowledge He gave me."

"I know. What I really meant was that if you hadn't come all the way down here from New York, my mother never would have had the new medicine you brought and would probably not be here now," Mandie said.

"You never know, but let's all be thankful that she has pulled through," Dr. Plumbley said.

"Yes, we're so thankful and so appreciative of your coming here, Dr. Plumbley," Mrs. Taft said.

"I was trying to catch you to let you know I'm getting ready to return to New York and I just wanted to tell you goodbye," the big doctor said, looking down at Mandie. "You see, I'm thankful, too, for the chance you gave me and my nephew, Missy."

Mandie knew he was talking about the big ruby she had given him a while back. The money from the ruby had helped further his medical education and helped start his nephew on his.

"How is Moses, Dr. Plumbley?" Mandie asked.

"He's fine. He's doing quite well in school. I'm proud of him. He'll probably make a better doctor than I am," Dr. Plumbley said with a big smile.

"Not in our opinion, Dr. Plumbley," Mrs. Taft said.

"Please come back soon, when you have some vacation time, and bring Moses with you next time," Mandie told him.

"I'll do that. Abraham has asked us to visit him and do nothing but go fishing, like in the old days," Dr. Plumbley said with a laugh. "And I think that's a great idea."

"I think so, too," Mandie said. Then she asked, "We forgot to ask Dr. Woodard when we could see my mother again. Can you tell us?"

"I would guess Dr. Woodard will limit your visits to twice a day, once in the morning and once in the afternoon, until she gets some strength back," Dr. Plumbley replied. "Now I have to rush. I have a train to catch."

"A train to catch? Why, the trains at this depot here don't even run on a schedule," Mandie told him. "I know because I went down there trying to find out when the train from New York would be coming in, and the man said just any old time, depending on where you changed and all that."

The big doctor laughed and said, "I know. Just like it was back in the old days when I lived here in Franklin. Only this time Abraham is at the depot and he says he'll hold the train till I get there. So let me get going now. I hope to see you all again soon."

Mandie and Mrs. Taft told the doctor goodbye and walked on down the hallway to Mandie's room. Mrs. Taft didn't go in but told Mandie she was going to her own room upstairs to rest for a while.

"And if you get any word from Dr. Woodard that we can see Elizabeth again, let me know, dear," Mrs. Taft said, going on down the hallway toward the stairs.

"I will, Grandmother," Mandie promised as she stepped into her room. Then she remembered Joe was supposed to wait on the window seat. She went back into the hallway. But Joe was not there.

"Well, I wonder where he is?" she remarked to herself.

She went back inside her room and sat down. She was still excited about seeing her mother. However, her mother didn't look good at all, and she was still worried about her.

Her thoughts were interrupted by the sudden appearance of Polly in her doorway. She got up and said, "Why, come on in, Polly. Have a seat."

Polly came in and sat down. "I just wanted to come and tell you I'm glad your mother is better," she said.

Mandie looked at her and asked, "Why, news sure does travel fast. When did you hear about my mother?"

"Just now," Polly said. "I was just going to check on

the tunnel exit and I ran smack into Joe. He told me."

"Joe was down at the tunnel exit? I wonder why?" Mandie asked.

"Well, he told me he was following some lady in a black dress and she disappeared," Polly said with a shrug.

"Following a lady in a black dress?" Mandie asked in surprise.

"That's what he said," Polly confirmed. "Of course, you know your house here is full of ladies in black dresses."

"I know. Where did Joe go, Polly?" Mandie asked.

"I don't know. I left him down at the tunnel exit when he told me your mother was better and that you had been able to see her," Polly replied.

"Come on. Let's go see if we can find him," Mandie said as she stood up.

"Well, if you insist," Polly agreed.

Mandie decided Polly just wanted to play hard-to-get as far as Joe was concerned.

The two girls went down the back stairs and out into the yard. They hurried down the hill to the tunnel exit. Joe was not in sight.

"I wonder where he could have gone?" Mandie remarked as she pushed back the bushes to check the tunnel door. It was locked.

"I have no idea," Polly said.

"Let's walk around and look for him," Mandie suggested.

"If you really want to, but I don't believe he's anywhere around here," Polly said.

Mandie stopped, looked at her, and asked, "Why do you say that?"

"Well, I figure if he was really chasing a lady in black, he'd keep on chasing her. He wouldn't be standing around down here somewhere," Polly said.

"You're absolutely right, Polly. We might as well go on back to the house," Mandie said.

They walked back up the hill and around the house to the front porch. There they found Joe sitting in the swing.

Mandie stopped and looked at him. "Well, did you catch the lady wearing black?"

Joe got up, laughed, and said, "No, she was too quick for me. Y'all come sit down and I'll tell you all about it."

When the two girls sat in the swing with him, he began his story. "You see, it was like this." He looked at Mandie. "As soon as you went off to visit your mother, I was sitting there quietly on the window seat and along comes this lady all dressed in black. She had a bonnet on and had her head bent with a handkerchief over her nose. And guess what? She was crying."

Mandie gasped and said, "Now you see, Joe, I didn't make all that up. I really did see such a woman."

"I didn't say you made it up," Joe told her. "I told you I didn't know how you'd ever find out who she was, or something like that. Anyway, she didn't even see me. So I decided to see where she was going." He paused.

"Well?" Mandie asked.

"I don't know that she was going any particular place, but she walked around the house and on down through the woods toward the tunnel exit. I lost her down there and that's when I ran into Polly," Joe explained.

"I didn't see any woman dressed in black," Polly commented.

"Remember the woods are thick and it's also a big place down there. Almost anyone could avoid you if they wanted to in those woods," Joe said.

"This is really a mystery," Mandie commented. "Did you think she looked like one of Aunt Dorabelle's daughters?"

"She was probably about the size of her daughters,

but I couldn't see her face so I don't know whether she was one of them or not," Joe said.

The three couldn't solve the mystery and had no idea as to how to continue. Polly had to go home and Mandie told Joe she should go to her room or see her grandmother to find out when she could visit her mother again.

"But it hasn't been long since you saw your mother, Mandie. I don't imagine you'll be able to visit her again so soon because she has been awfully sick," Joe said as they walked around the house.

"At least I'll go find out," Mandie told him. She entered the back entrance and Joe wandered off through the yard in search of Uncle Ned to see if he needed any help.

Mandie went straight up to her grandmother's room. Mrs. Taft was lying on the settee.

"Come on in, dear," Mrs. Taft told her, starting to get up as Mandie stuck her head in the doorway.

"Now, don't get up, Grandmother. I just wanted to ask if you've found out when we can see my mother again," Mandie said as she stepped inside the room.

Mrs. Taft, sitting up by now, said, "Dr. Woodard says not until tomorrow morning, dear, and I suppose he's right. So we'll just have to be patient."

"Oh, shucks!" Mandie said with a sigh. "Well, I'm going back to my room. Are you coming down to eat supper with me later?"

"Yes, dear, I'll be there," Mrs. Taft said as she lay back down.

Mandie went back to her room and sat around thinking about things again. She wondered what her mother would say about her little brother when she was able to talk more. Mandie would be glad when that was over.

Joe and Mrs. Taft had supper with Mandie in her room that night, and when Mandie said she wanted to rest and go to bed early, her grandmother and Joe left.

Mandie did go to bed early that night, but she tossed and turned with so much on her mind. The guilt she felt over Samuel's death was heaviest of all. Snowball kept protesting as she pulled the covers and displaced him. Finally she drifted off to sleep.

Later that night the angel returned. Mandie awoke, looked up and saw the angel standing by the side of her bed. She raised up on her elbow and waited for it to speak. Snowball huffed himself up behind her. She heard the clock strike three.

Because the radiant vision stood there without speaking, Mandie decided to say something.

"I thank you with all my heart for bringing me the message that night. You said that I would know," she said. "I finally did know what you meant. I wired for Dr. Plumbley to come from New York and he did, and you must know, if you're an angel, that he doctored my mother and she is on the way to recovery this very minute." She paused, waiting for a response.

The vision finally spoke in a quiet voice, "I did not come for your thanks. I came to tell you about your little brother, Samuel. You are forgiven for being jealous of him. God does not hold grudges. God decided it was time for Samuel to leave this earth. Samuel had something very painful wrong with him and was suffering from that when he caught the fever. Now you must get rid of your feelings of guilt and trust in God to heal your mother. Peace, my child."

With the last words, the vision seemed to evaporate as it had done the other time. The room darkened when the angel's light was gone.

A sob caught in Mandie's throat as she thought about what the angel had said. A warm feeling filled her body as she realized she was not responsible for her little brother's death. God had forgiven her. The angel had told her so. Now she could go back to sleep in peace.

When morning came, Mandie awoke and sat up in bed as she thought about the night before. Had an angel really come to visit her or had she dreamed it? She knew God had angels, but did He send them down to talk to people in times of trouble? She knew she had been worrying about what her mother would say regarding her little brother's death.

Mandie swung her feet out from under the sheet and sat on the side of the big bed. "I think I've been worrying about something that should have never bothered me. I don't believe God would take Samuel away from us because I was jealous of him, not really," she said aloud.

Snowball jumped off the bed and began prowling around the room.

"But then, did God really send one of His angels to talk to me about it, or did I just dream it because I had a guilty conscience?" she pondered.

She stood up and started looking for clothes to put on.

"I remember that dream in London when I heard Samuel crying so hard and then I heard my mother scream," she went on aloud. "That seemed so real when I woke up, but it was only a dream. So maybe that angel was in a dream, too."

She pulled a dress down from the chifferobe.

"Whether it was a dream or not I'll never know, but I do know I feel so much better this morning," she said as she pulled back the drapery to let the sunshine in. "And I hope my mother is, too."

Chapter 12 / Mysteries Unfold

Elizabeth rapidly improved and Dr. Woodard finally allowed Mandie to go to her mother's side. Uncle John had been with Elizabeth and he smiled at Mandie as he left the room.

"You may go in and hold your mother's hand if you want to this morning, Miss Amanda," Dr. Woodard told Mandie as she and her grandmother stood in the hallway outside Elizabeth's room.

"Thank you, Dr. Woodard!" Mandie cried and rushed inside the room.

Dr. Woodard looked at Mrs. Taft and said as he closed the door, "We need to keep this private, don't you think? You'll have your turn this afternoon."

Mandie ran to her mother's bed and gently took her hand. "Oh, Mother, I've been waiting so long to do this. I love you so much! I just can't tell you how much!" she cried. She buried her face in her mother's shoulder.

"You don't have to tell me. I know, Amanda," Elizabeth said, softly stroking Mandie's blonde hair. "Dr. Woodard says I'll be able to get up and about pretty soon. There's something I want you to do with me, dear."

Mandie raised her head, wiped the tears of joy from her face, and asked, "What, Mother? Anything that you want."

"This won't be easy to do," Elizabeth began, holding Mandie's hand in both of hers. "I've been lying here thinking about it during this whole time. You see, when your little brother died, I got sick and I was not able to be at the funeral. I would like for just you and me to go across the road and let me see his grave. Is that asking too much?" She looked at Mandie sadly.

Mandie tightened her grip on her mother's hand as she said, "No, Mother, that's not asking too much. I want to go with you." Her voice trembled. "Mother, I'm so sorry about Samuel. I really and truly loved him."

"I know you did, dear," Elizabeth said. "After you left for Europe, Dr. Woodard called in a specialist to find out why he cried so much and, Amanda," her voice also trembled, "he was suffering terrible pain from a back problem. The doctors said he would never have any relief and would never grow up to be normal. So he's out of his pain now. And we can't be selfish enough to want him back here where he suffered." She took a deep breath.

"I know, Mother. Joe told me but I didn't believe him. And you know, Mother, an angel came to visit me," Mandie said softly.

"Oh, Amanda, an angel?" her mother asked in surprise.

"Yes, ma'am, and it explained all this to me," Mandie said in almost a whisper. "It had come to see me one night before that and told me I would know what to do, and I decided I should wire for Dr. Plumbley to come."

"God works in mysterious ways, Amanda," Elizabeth said, smiling at her daughter. "Tell me all about this, dear."

Mandie explained to her mother how the angel had appeared twice and that she didn't know whether the angel was real or was only in a dream.

"Whichever way it was, dear, it came from God," Elizabeth said.

"The appearance of the angel reminded me of a poem I learned in the fourth grade called 'Abou Ben Adhem.' It went like this: 'Abou Ben Adhem, may his tribe increase, awoke one night from a deep dream of peace and saw within the moonlight in his room, making it rich, and like a lily in bloom, an angel writing in a book of gold . . .' The angel appeared like that to me and it made the room brighter than daylight," Mandie told her.

"I would imagine so, dear," her mother said.

"It was like the angel had a secret and wanted me to share it," Mandie said. "And whether it was real or not, I'll always be thankful."

Dr. Woodard quietly opened the door and said, "Visiting time is up. We don't want to overdo it."

Mandie hugged her mother one more time and then stood up, still holding her hand. "I have to let you rest now so you can regain your strength and we can do things together, Mother," Mandie said, smiling down at her.

"Soon, dear," Elizabeth told her.

Mandie was light-headed with happiness.

That day Mrs. Taft talked to Mandie about the visiting kinpeople.

"I think we ought to go down and have one meal with them, dear," Mrs. Taft said. "I understand they will begin going home tomorrow and we really haven't been very hospitable."

"Yes, I can face them now, even with all the questions they are bound to ask," Mandie agreed.

That afternoon, Uncle John finally left his watch at

Elizabeth's bed and came downstairs. Everyone gathered around the dining table for supper that night. Mandie found everyone to be friendly and not too "nosey," as Liza had classified them. Dr. Woodard had given permission to Aunt Dorabelle and her two daughters to visit Elizabeth, which they had done that afternoon.

"I thank all of you for coming when we needed you so badly," Mandie said, looking around the table. "I know I haven't been very sociable, but now that the worry is gone about my mother, I realize how important you all were to us with your prayers and other help."

Uncle John spoke up, "Yes, and I add my deepest thanks. You must all come back soon."

"Why, we're kinpeople, after all," Aunt Dorabelle said. "And, Amanda, we understand how upset you were about your mother and brother. Maybe when Elizabeth is able, you will all come to visit us."

Aunt Dorabelle took over the conversation and her two daughters only smiled at Mandie. The other relatives were quiet, since her aunt didn't allow them to "git a word in crossways," as Liza described it to Mandie later.

"We'll be leaving tomorrow afternoon," Mandie heard Aunt Dorabelle tell her grandmother. Liza stood nearby, rolling her eyes.

From the other side of the room, a loud voice commanded, "Liza, git dem plates off dat table and bring in de sweet stuff."

Mandie turned, and seeing Aunt Lou, she jumped up, almost turning over her chair, and ran to hug the woman. Aunt Lou had been busy with Mandie's mother, and Mandie had not been able to catch up with her.

"Oh, Aunt Lou!" Mandie cried as the woman held her tight.

"No, my chile, dis ain't no way to act in front o' comp'ny," Aunt Lou said.

"Aunt Lou, I haven't seen you since my mother moved into the other room. Where have you been?" Mandie asked, looking up at the old woman.

"My chile, I had a small case o' sniffles and dat doctuh man say it be best fo' me to stay 'way from yo' mother. I been at Abraham and Jenny's house fo' a few days. But now I'm well, and I say you git back to de table and act like a lady," Aunt Lou said, smiling down at her as she held her at arm's length.

Abraham, Uncle John's yardman, and his wife, Jenny, the cook, lived in a small house in the backyard. It had been provided for them by Mandie's grandfather before he died. And Mandie realized now that she had not been to see them either.

"I'm almost finished eating, Aunt Lou," Mandie said. "I've got to visit with all of you soon."

"I'se gotta go now and let Dr. Woodard come down heah and eat," Aunt Lou said as she left the room and Mandie returned to the table.

"Dr. Woodard is so dedicated to his patients. Even though Elizabeth is so much better, he won't leave her unattended for a moment," Mrs. Taft remarked.

"Well, we're almost kinpeople," Joe said, with a big smile.

Mandie looked at Uncle Ned, smiled, and said, "So is Uncle Ned. Even though he is not blood kin, I love him like a real uncle. He was my father's friend."

"Jim Shaw like brother," Uncle Ned said to her.

Mandie noticed that the kinpeople didn't seem to know what to think of a real Cherokee Indian being a guest in her house. She was sure they all knew she was part Cherokee, too. Maybe that's why they were all so formal and aloof.

When the meal was over, Mandie and Joe went to sit

in the swing on the front porch. The sky had been overcast and it soon became dark.

Mandie was in good spirits. "Let's do something dangerous," she teased with a big smile. She stopped the motion of the swing with her foot.

"Dangerous, like what?" Joe asked.

She thought for a moment and said, "Like going through the tunnel after dark."

"Well, if you remember, the tunnel is always dark whether it's dark outside or not," Joe said.

"I know, but it's always daytime when we come out of the exit in the woods. Let's be brave and go through the tunnel out into the dark woods," she suggested.

"Well, I suppose we could," Joe said as he stood up. "I'll have to get the keys from Mr. Bond—and a lantern."

"You get the lantern and I'll get the keys," Mandie told him.

Mandie found Mr. Bond in the kitchen talking to Aunt Lou. He was surprised when Mandie asked for the keys and told him she and Joe were going through the tunnel.

"You sure you want to go through that dark place at night?" he asked as he wrestled a bunch of keys out of his pocket, selected two, and handed them to Mandie.

"I'm not afraid. If I don't bring these keys back within an hour or so, you come looking for us, will you?" Mandie said with a laugh as she took the keys.

"I imagine the whole house will be huntin' you by then, Missy," he said. "Now, do be careful. Be sure Joe has extra matches with him."

Mandie met Joe at the bottom of the stairs to the third floor. He had a lantern and a pocketful of matches.

The third floor was quiet and there seemed to be no one around. They walked softly to the door of Uncle

John's library and Mandie inserted the key in the lock. Joe lit the lantern.

As the door to the library swung open and the light from the lantern illuminated the room, Mandie was shocked to see a woman in black with a lighted candle in her hand, standing before the portrait of her Cherokee grandmother that hung over the mantelpiece. And the woman was equally shocked to see them. She turned as they entered the room and Mandie saw that it was Isabelle, Aunt Dorabelle's elder daughter.

"Well," Mandie said in surprise.

"So you are Amanda," Isabelle said, quickly averting her gaze.

Mandie gasped. Here was the voice that had been saying, "So you are Amanda" all along.

"Why do you keep saying 'So you are Amanda'?" Mandie asked as they all stood there in the light from the lantern. Mandie could now see that Isabelle had been crying.

"It's a long story, Amanda, and I don't really know where to begin," Isabelle said in a husky voice as she extinguished the candle and set it on a table nearby. "You see, you should have been mine."

Mandie's eyes flew wide open. "What are you talking about?" she asked as she held her breath.

"Let's sit down over here," Isabelle told Mandie. "You, too, Joe, because I know how close you are to Amanda." She led the way to the ornate couch on the other side of the room and they all sat down.

"You've been crying," Mandie blurted out in spite of herself. "I saw you in the room down the hallway one day and you were crying then, too."

"My tears would float a battleship, my dear," Isabelle said as she reached to touch Mandie's blonde hair. "The only way I know how to tell this is just to say I was in love with your father, Amanda, and your mother, Elizabeth, came along and stole his heart, and I've never recovered." She sighed loudly.

Mandie began to withdraw from the woman. "You hold a grudge against my mother?" she asked.

"Oh, no, dear, not at all. I could see that Jim didn't love me, so I never protested when he married Elizabeth. Of course my heart has been silently mourning the loss of him to my cousin, but no one ever knew how much it hurt me," Isabelle said.

Mandie couldn't quite comprehend all that Isabelle was telling her. This must have all taken place at least fourteen years ago, but Isabelle was still crying over it. How could anyone cry over a lost love for that many years?

"I came here with my mother just to see you. I don't know how much you know of your background, but you were born in my mother's house," Isabelle said.

Mandie gasped again. She had never thought to ask where she had actually been born. "In Aunt Dorabelle's house?" she asked.

"Yes, and Joe's father delivered you into this world," Isabelle added.

Joe spoke for the first time and said, "I always figured he had by things I hear now and then."

Mandie jumped up and walked around the room. "This is just too much to take in at one time," she said. Turning back to Isabelle, she asked, "If my mother took my father away from you, why did she decide to go to your mother's house to have me?"

"Oh, but there's never been any hard feelings between Elizabeth and me, or with your father," Isabelle said. "I got one last chance to see him when he came to my mother's house to take you away. You know, of course, that your grandmother told him that your mother didn't want you, and she told Elizabeth that you had died."

"Oh, yes, I learned about that a long time ago," Mandie said. She walked across the room and came back to stand in front of Isabelle. "If you loved my father so much, why did you get married to another man. You must be married, or have been married, because you have a different name from your mother's." Mandie sat down again.

"Amanda, when I saw there was no hope for me, and Jim married Elizabeth, I didn't want to become an old maid, so I married Dorsey Evins. He was an old childhood friend who was always determined he was going to marry me," Isabelle explained with a sad look on her face.

"So where is he?" Mandie asked.

"Dear, he drowned the day after we were married. We had been to church, and coming home we had to cross an old bridge. We had had lots of rain, so the bridge was weak, but we didn't know it. The carriage went into the river when the bridge fell, but I can't swim," she said with tears in her eyes. "Dorsey was a good swimmer and he rescued me from the wreckage and put me on a dry spot on a large rock. He went back to save our kitten who was tangled in the mess."

She paused and Mandie knew what was coming next. She felt tears in her own eyes.

"He was a white kitten, just like yours, and someone had given him to us when they learned we were getting married," Isabelle explained. "Dorsey got trapped in the wrecked carriage and went down with it while I was watching." Her voice trembled.

Mandie reached to pat her hand. "I'm sorry," she said. "And I'm sorry you loved my father and couldn't have him."

Isabelle didn't say anything for a few minutes. Then she got up, shook out her long skirts, and withdrew two keys from her pocket. "Here, I should give these to you. I have no right to keep them. These are the keys to the library and the tunnel that your father gave me when we were ... in love ... before he met Elizabeth." She held out two golden keys.

Mandie looked at the keys in her hand and shook her head. "No, no, I wouldn't take those for anything. My father gave them to you and they belong to you," she said as she, too, stood up.

Isabelle looked hard at Mandie for a moment and Mandie quickly threw her arms around Isabelle. Her father had loved this woman, and this woman still loved her father after all these years. Isabelle hugged Mandie tight.

Joe broke up the scene as he asked, "Well, are we going through the tunnel or not?"

"It's probably too late, don't you think? Mr. Jason may come searching for us if we're not back with the keys soon," Mandie said as she backed off from Isabelle and straightened her skirts.

Isabelle looked at the keys in her hand and slowly put them back into her pocket. "I'll keep these if you insist," she said. "I've never been back in this house all these years until Elizabeth became sick, and goodness knows when I'll ever return."

"Let's go," Joe said, picking up the lantern.

They all walked down the stairs together and met Uncle Ned at the bottom of the steps.

"Mother of Papoose want to see Papoose," Uncle Ned told Mandie.

"She does?" Mandie said as she left the others and ran down the hallway to her mother's bedroom. Elizabeth had been moved back into her own room as she had become better.

Mandie found her and Uncle John sitting on the settee in their sitting room.

"Mother, Uncle Ned said you wanted to see me, and here you are, sitting up on the settee. I'm so glad you're better," Mandie said as she went to her mother's side.

Uncle Ned had followed her and he now stood in the doorway.

"Yes, dear, I'm much better, and I want you to do me a favor," Elizabeth said as Mandie sat on a footstool nearby.

"Anything, Mother," Mandie told her.

"I want you to go home with Uncle Ned and visit with Sallie awhile. You'll soon have to be going back to school and you need a little vacation away from this house," Elizabeth told her.

Mandie began protesting. "No, Mother, I want to stay here with you every minute until I have to leave for school."

"Amanda, I'm worried about you getting some rest and relaxation," Elizabeth insisted. "You've been through some trying times. Now, if you'll do this for me I'll feel better about it all, too."

"Well," Mandie slowly began. "I suppose I could go stay a day or two. I'd like to tell Sallie about Europe." She quickly looked at Uncle John, who was smiling at her. "Is that what you want me to do, too, Uncle John?"

"Of course, dear, I agree on anything your mother wants," he said.

Mandie laughed and teased him, "You're going to spoil her, you know."

Elizabeth laughed at that, and it was good for Mandie to hear her mother laugh again. They had been to visit Samuel's grave that morning with Uncle John's assistance. Her mother had been completely torn up when she saw the little tombstone with Samuel's name on it. Mandie had tried to hold back her own grief and help her mother. So now Mandie was willing to forget her own wishes and do what her mother desired.

Mandie looked up at Uncle Ned in the doorway and asked, "When do we leave, Uncle Ned?"

"Crack of dawn, Papoose," he said. "Sallie anxious to see you. She send word Tsa'ni also anxious to see you."

"Tsa'ni?" Mandie repeated the name. Tsa'ni was the Cherokee boy who was always making trouble for other people. "I wonder what he wants to see me for? He doesn't even like me."

"Sallie say important," Uncle Ned said.

Mandie sighed and said, "Well, if Sallie says it's important, then it must be."

"Morning Star go home days ago," Uncle Ned said.

Mandie had been so wrapped up in her own problems that she had forgotten about Morning Star having been there. "I'm sorry, Uncle Ned, I just haven't kept up with everything," she said.

"Now go pack a few things, dear, and be sure you take enough to last a few days," Elizabeth said.

"Are you sure you'll be all right without me around?" Mandie asked, anxiously looking at her mother.

Elizabeth smiled and said, "Of course, dear. Your uncle John is here to see that I am."

"Well, I guess I'll have to go pack then," Mandie said slowly.

She didn't really want to leave her mother, but she did want to see Uncle Ned's granddaughter, Sallie, who lived with the old man and Morning Star.

Besides, she could smell a mystery a mile away. And Tsa'ni's message seemed to hold a secret. Well, she'd soon find out whether this was just another one of the tricks Tsa'ni was constantly playing on others.